Littlest Blessings

Edited By Lynn C. Johnston

A Whispering Angel Book

Littlest Blessings

ISBN **978-0-9841421-8-7**

Whispering Angel Books
7557 West Sand Lake Road #126
Orlando, FL 32819

http://www.whisperingangelbooks.com

Printed in the United States of America

A rose can say "I love you",
orchids can enthrall,
but a weed bouquet in a chubby fist,
yes, that says it all.

~Author Unknown

TABLE OF CONTENTS

DEDICATION

This book is dedicated to all of the children who have touched our lives. Thank you for sharing your unconditional love, boundless imagination, and unbridled curiosity. You are truly a blessing to all of us.

ACKNOWLEDGMENTS

The creation and development of this book would not have been possible without the assistance of many people. I would like to thank everyone who submitted their heartfelt stories and poems for this anthology. With hundreds of wonderful pieces to choose from, each prospective contributor made the selection process far more challenging and rewarding than imaginable.

My deepest appreciation goes out to Julie G. Beers, Bob Bergstrom and Salina Bergstrom. Their opinions, support, and expertise were invaluable during this process.

INTRODUCTION

Jackie Kennedy once said, "The children have been a wonderful gift to me, and I'm thankful to have once again seen our world through their eyes."

As anyone who has ever loved a child knows, children are an amazing gift. They enter into the world knowing nothing about life, but yet somehow manage to teach us the true meaning of it. Through their eyes, we are able to see the world with a renewed perspective where love is unconditional, imagination and curiosity are limitless, and resilience from adversity seems endless.

No matter their age, our children are both our greatest and littlest blessings. In this anthology, you'll read about the joy and wonderment they bring into our lives, and the enduring lessons they teach us when we least expect it.

I'll never forget the first lesson I learned from my son, Sam. When I learned I was pregnant, I was scared. I was a 30-year-old single woman and I knew this unplanned pregnancy would come as a shock to my friends and family, and an unwelcome surprise to my boyfriend of three years. Despite all of my apprehension at becoming a single mother, I was overjoyed at the thought of bringing a new life into the world.

My pregnancy was difficult with several months of morning sickness, aches and pains, and hormonally-driven mood swings. As my abdomen grew bigger, so did my concerns over the next stage of my life. I had wanted to be a mother ever since I was a young girl playing with my baby dolls, but I hadn't dreamed of doing it without a husband.

After a long labor, my son was finally delivered by C-section. I saw him for a brief moment before they whisked him away for his examination. As I rested in the recovery room, it still seemed like the whole thing was just a dream. It wasn't until he was brought to me a couple of hours later that the reality of my new life – and my new role – set in.

When he was first laid in my arms, his half-opened eyes met mine. I gently unwrapped his swaddling blanket and felt his tiny hand. In that moment, a song broke out of the archives of my mind: *He Touched Me,* sung beautifully by Barbra Streisand. The lyrics celebrate a sudden and profound love that changes her life forever.

The music and lyrics played in my mind as my heart swelled at the sight of my new son. It was the perfect song to express my feelings. I did feel a *sudden tingle, a sparkle, a glow.* He *was real* and the world *was alive and shining.* And I did feel that *wonderful drive toward valentining* – all because *he touched me.*

As I looked at my brand-new son, I knew at that moment that my life really had changed forever. And, as it said in the song, I knew nothing would ever be the same. I learned in that moment that despite the difficulties in my pregnancy and the challenges we would face in the future, everything would be okay as long as we were together.

My son is almost grown now. It's hard to believe he'll be off to college next year and then starting a life of his own. While I have spent his life trying to teach him all of the things he'll need to succeed, I can't help but know that he has taught me even more. I don't think there is a day that has gone by that he hasn't taught me something about love, courage, compassion – or even about my own relationship with my parents.

As you read these heartfelt stories and poems, I hope you will reflect on your own special memories of the children in your life and remember that children are our littlest blessings and our greatest gift of all.

~ Lynn C. Johnston

MENTORING TOMAS
By Carolyn T. Johnson

Tomas swaggered up to my waiting Jeep and opened the back door. He still sat in the back seat on the way to the movies even though he was now fifteen years old and five-foot-three. His hair was gelled forward and his cheap cologne filled the air with a pungent, sweet smell. Seems like overnight he'd become a young man.

I still remember our first meeting six years ago. He was a shy little third grader whose teacher had signed him up for the mentoring program in his elementary school. The look on his face showed obvious disappointment at being paired with an older Anglo lady and I was at a loss for where to start. The notes from his teacher said he never smiled, so my initial goal was to make him laugh.

We'd meet for an hour every Wednesday afternoon at school. Sometimes we'd review class work, but a lot of times we'd just play cards or do word puzzles. I'd always bring him bottled water and a snack for our hour together. He wasn't much of a talker but, little by little, I coaxed information out of him. His mother had left him and his big brother with his grandmother in Mexico until she found work in Texas. According to Tomas, his father didn't even know he existed. His mom remarried and had two more children. They all lived in a cramped little apartment in walking distance from the school.

When his tenth birthday rolled around, I mailed him a card with a twenty dollar bill in it and invited him to join me for lunch at the McDonalds down the street from his apartment. He walked into the fast food chain, proud as punch, with his brand new birthday money pinned to his t-shirt.

When Tomas finished fourth grade, the mentoring program moved on to a new school district. I didn't feel right being a dedicated friend for two years then disappearing, so I gave Tomas my phone number. The first time he called, we went to a movie. He was frightened of the elevator, so we took the stairs to the box office. I gave him the money to pay for our tickets and popcorn. He asked a million questions. He'd never been to a movie theater before.

Movie theaters weren't the only thing new for him. The first time we went to a sit-down restaurant for pizza, he didn't have a clue what to do. I showed him the menu and had him tell the waitress what he wanted. Then I made him figure out how much money we owed and explained why you leave a tip.

Another time, I took him to a popular hotdog place. He ordered a hamburger and fries because he didn't know what a hotdog was, much less tater tots.

For his twelfth birthday, we ventured into Toys-R-Us. I handed him a twenty dollar bill and told him to pick out anything in the store. His eyes were big as saucers. He had never seen such an amazing array of toys. We spent two hours going up and down the aisles touching each and every action figure until he found the three he really wanted.

Once, my husband and I even treated him to an NBA game downtown. He'd lived most of his life ten minutes away but had never been downtown among all the tall buildings. When we got into the stadium, his jaw dropped. After loading up on hot dogs and drinks, we made our way down to our seats. The poor child was star-struck. He never left his seat during the game, not even to go to the bathroom.

During our many excursions over the past six years, we've talked about how kids who don't have any friends join gangs, how sad it was that his big brother had to spend eighteen months in jail for stealing a car and how he'd have a hard time getting a job when he got out. We even touched on immigration when the INS questioned his stepdad.

At the cash register at Baskin Robbins one day, Tomas saw a small sign with a dollar bill on it that said *watch for counterfeits*. That launched the discussion of what a counterfeit bill was and why it was wrong to make them. We've even had talks about college because he mentioned his mom had wanted his older brother to go to college. I explained what doors open when you have a college degree.

In the midst of his teenage years, Tomas still calls to get together but is less talkative than before and walks a few steps behind me. Conversations are like pulling teeth. At some point, he will decide it is no longer cool to hang with someone my age and our relationship will change or maybe he'll just disappear. I may never get to see him graduate, get his first promotion, or start a family, but what gives me great solace is knowing I've planted the seed of opportunity in him.

JUST ASK
By Cona F. Gregory-Adams

The world is full of little
tykes, waiting to be heard.
All you need do is listen,
they'll gladly give the word.

You may not understand
just how their logic works,
but if you listen closely
you'll laugh until it hurts.

The highlight of my talk
with any little sprout,
toss in a simple question,
see what comes back out.

My nephew came to visit;
I took him round the farm,
introduced him to the animals,
as we strolled through the barn.

His eyes lit up when I asked
if he could tell me how
to keep the milk from spoiling;
he said, "Keep it in the cow."

WHEN DID I WEEP?
By Elayne Clift

Not when I hugged you goodbye
at a college dormitory,
a frightened, wide-eyed innocent;

Not when I waved you farewell
at a crowded airport,
Paris-bound, an ingénue;

Not when I watched you saunter
down the aisle, a grinning
strong, new graduate;

But when I blew you a kiss
one ordinary Sunday
as you drove away from home.

For then did I know --
the cutting of the cord
had come,

and that your sweet life
is everywhere you are...
but here.

LUNCHROOM LESSONS
By Lynn Pinkerton

If I were Queen, I would mandate that at least twice each year every adult would have lunch at the school cafeteria with a small shining child of their choice. Something happens when you dutifully check in at the front office of the school, stride through hallways proudly flaunting wild explosions of fresh knowledge and head toward the long-forgotten aromas of the school cafeteria. Tumbling stock market jitters and traffic aggravations and deadlines and CNN Breaking News and new gray hairs and mortgage uncertainties meekly turn tail and sulk timidly away. Adult frets and worries are no match for quiet halls softly echoing with tender evidence of what is really important in life. I was reminded of this phenomenon recently when I grabbed a McDonald's Happy Meal and set off to the local elementary school to have lunch with Kara, my six-year-old niece.

Kara greeted me with arms flung open in joyous wild abandon. Giant cartwheels leap-frogged through my heart so unrestrained I looked to see if anyone had noticed. When I eased down to sit at the short, green oval table ringed with eight untarnished, kindergarten faces, life somehow became simple and comforting.

Cutting through petty pomp and circumstance, one short clear-eyed lad immediately announced to me that he had a girlfriend. I asked him how he knew she was his girlfriend. He got up and came around to whisper in my ear, "She kissed me right on my lips." To seal his confession, he held up a tiny wisp of brown finger and said we had to pinky-swear that I would not divulge his secret. His plucky act reminded me that sometimes it is best to boldly trust your gut when you meet a new friend and need to share what is on your mind.

Two pig-tailed girls across from me announced that they were "BFF...best friends forever" and asked if I wanted to be best friends with them. A blond pixie of a boy at the next table leaned over and asked if I could come to his house after school and play cars, and a hazel-eyed, snaggle-toothed girl shyly invited me to her birthday party on Saturday. While I mulled over the offers, a freckled faced, Huck Finn sort of boy next to me, whispered reassuringly, "Since you're the new lady, I'll hold your hand when we leave, so you won't be scared."

Squeaks, squeals and secret-sharing rose in volume and prompted a rosy-cheeked teacher to stand up and raise her hand, index finger pointing skyward. One by one, a wave of unsteady stillness washed over the cavernous room as small arms of every color climbed above short heads like slender flags signaling silence. Kara whispered to me this sign meant we had gotten too loud and now had to "be quieter and listen better to what each other had to say." I had only been a resident of this small community table for twenty minutes and already I felt my perspective shifting into clearer focus.

Having grown up a lifetime member of the "clean plate club," I offered my niece's untouched cheese and crackers to a young man at our table who kept eyeing them. I was quickly reprimanded by a chorus of small voices telling me that we don't share food because "we care about our friends and we don't want them to catch our germs." Seems I had a lot to learn.

Half an hour after being swept up into this gentle, innocent vortex of compassion and acceptance, someone somewhere gave a sign and small feet and hands scurried to clean up lunch, leave it like they found it and line up at the door. I offered my sad farewells amid their hugs and pleas to come back tomorrow and "sit by me." Humbled, I watched my new, pint-sized friends march single file out the door and into their unfurling lives. I turned and marched back into my own life, grateful and restored.

MADE VISIBLE
For Kate
By Deb Sherrer

Small silver crests peak and roll
on a lake bordered
by rustling, sun-tipped pines,
while the black wings of crow slice blue sky.

Long strands of brunette hair lift, float
framing dark chocolate eyes
brushing rose-tinted lips
her ripening body supine, in rhythm
with the gentle roll of
the sun-bleached dock.

Walking away
her hand seeks mine,
nestles, then stays —
a moment at 12, almost 50
daughter and mother
the wind
the love
made visible.

TWILIGHT *PAS DE DEUX*
By Ann Reisfeld Boutté

From my kitchen window
I watch my neighbor
return from work
at twilight.
His three-year-old
runs to meet him.
He sweeps her up
and lifts her
overhead across the
sunset. They twirl,
they laugh. He lowers
her gently. She leaps
in one direction, then
another. He follows closely
but never overtakes her.
She extends her arms
to him and he dissolves
into smiles. Another
lift, another spin before
they exit behind the door.

With each performance,
I relive the pairings
with my own sons,
now grown. How
sweet the music, how
brief the dance.

GIANT BLACK WIDOW SPIDER ISLAND
By Julie G. Beers

Giant Black Widow Spider Island loomed in the distance. Despite my terror, Bijan steered our ship in that direction. I tried to get Sophia to stop him but she jumped off the ship and ran onto the island, ready for battle.

I'm not a big fan of bugs. Spiders are definitely not on my list of favorites and Giant Black Widow Spiders are the absolute worst. But I had my 6 year old nephew and my 3½ year old niece to protect me so slowly I got off our ship.

The island bore a suspicious resemblance to my brother Dan's backyard so we knew these giant spiders were smart and were trying to trick us. The Giant Black Widows came at us fast and furious. They came from behind bushes, climbed over rooftops and dropped from trees. It seemed everywhere I ran a Giant Black Widow was trying to kill me. I wasn't very good at killing them but thankfully Bijan and Sophia dispatched them easily. In a few minutes the island was quiet – all the spiders were dead.

Our mission accomplished, the three of us climbed back on our ship and set sail. I was pretty worn out from our battle but Bijan coolly informed me we weren't done for the day. We were going to Dinosaur, Spider and Flies Island – but not to worry, the flies were good. Not to worry?! What about the Dinosaurs and the Spiders? We'd been to Tyrannosaurus Rex Island before but this was different – this was all kinds of dinosaurs.

"No," said Bijan. "Not all kinds, just the meat eating ones."

"What? They think we're meat!"

Bijan and Sophia laughed. They were confident in their powers. "Besides," said Bijan, "I've turned into a cheetah!" Bijan's sharp claws and cheetah growl got ready to attack.

"And I'm a vampire bat," announced Sophia.

"What can I be?" I wondered.

"You're a yak," decided Bijan.

"A yak? I'm a yak?"

Sophia giggled as Bijan nodded.

"Can't I be a giraffe?"

"Nope, you're a yak. But you can have a horn," Bijan said generously.

"Great," I was excited.

"But I kill all the meat eating monsters," said Bijan, raising his cheetah claws again. "You can only use your horn to stab the ones that don't eat meat."

"But there are only meat eating monsters on this island, right?"

"Yup," Bijan laughed as he jumped off the ship and onto the island.

Sophia giggled and followed her brother onto the island. Once again I was the last one off the boat but this time I had a good excuse. I was a yak and surely they didn't move very fast.

Bijan was cheetah clawing monsters all over the island and Sophia was flying above everything, occasionally zooming in for a vampire bite. Let me tell you, this was one monster packed island.

"It's too scary here," I cried. "I don't think we're going to be able to get them all, do you?"

Bijan stopped mid-cheetah claw. "Aunt Julie, you know it's just pretend."

"Really?" I looked stunned for a moment, and then suddenly smiled at him. "If it's just pretend, how come there's a giant spider crawling over the garage roof right behind you?"

Bijan smiled back at me then turned around and took down that spider with a mighty swipe of his claws.

"Back to the ship," yelled Sophia.

"We're going to Giant Bug Island now," said Bijan as he climbed aboard.

"I don't want to be a yak there. I want to be a vampire bat like Sophia." Sophia nodded and smiled at me.

"Okay," said Bijan. "But you're a zombie too."

"Cool." I was now a vampire zombie bat going to Giant Bug Island. I'm not sure how many monsters a vampire zombie can take down but that's okay. Bijan and Sophia would save me as they saved the day.

MY LITTLE SUPERSTAR
By Lynn C. Johnston

He takes the stage and holds the mic
Close up to his lips
He sings of love both lost and found
As he bumps and grinds his hips

But he doesn't have a record deal
Or albums made of gold
He's just my singing superstar
Who's all of five years old

His stage: atop a full size bed
His spot: an old flashlight
He dances in the mirror
As I gleam with such delight

His songs: taped off the radio
And a few he learned from me
He works so hard to learn the words
And tries to sing in key

His costume: that's the topper
As he belts out to his tape
Superman pajamas,
Complete with feet and cape

He is my little superstar
Who knows where this will go
But for a singing five-year-old
He puts on quite a show

A PRAYER
By Jason Miller

Most girls host
lemonade stands
(of course) and
some boys use
cardboard boxes
to build a
rock museum
where they charge
for tours.

But near the shore
your children
built a snowman
made of sand —
asking God to
calm the tide
so he won't
melt into the ocean.

THE MAGIC IN GREEN INK AND RED FOIL STARS
By R'becca Groff

There is an inner-city program in my city called the Matthew 25 Ministry that works to help marginalized children and their families realize a better life. This program has its roots in the United Methodist Church and is based on the scripture in the 25th Chapter of the book Matthew:

Jesus said, "I was hungry and you gave me food to eat. I was thirsty and you gave me a drink. I was a stranger and you welcomed me. I was naked and you gave me clothes to wear. I was sick and you took care of me. I was in prison and you visited me."

The program was started with the belief that there is more that unites caring people than divides them, and that one of the most powerful ways to bring people together is through service, and that everyone in a community is gifted, even the ones that oftentimes get labeled as needy.

To that end I spent 40 minutes every Tuesday afternoon as a Matthew 25 tutor working and reading with a first grade boy in one of our elementary schools located in a stressed neighborhood.

We had a packet that had been designed for us by the program coordinator at that particular school that contained word cards, word games and a workbook in which the child could practice his reading and writing.

I'd been working with this boy since for nearly 6 months, and things had been going fairly "swimmingly" until early spring when his attention seemed to have faded. It was highly possible that the antsy-pantsies of early spring fever had set in, but I had my doubts in this particular case. All of a sudden a boy who had been willing to read the word cards, and even after not too much coaxing, would write some sentences--didn't want to do much of anything. He seemed to prefer dropping his word cards down the crevice in the lunch room table we worked at, taking a good bit of time diving under said table to retrieve the pencil—whose lead he'd bust at least twice per session, eventually just laying his head down saying, "I don't want to . . ." to just about everything I tried to do with him.

This wasn't going to work for either of us if it kept on.

We volunteers go in as just that: volunteers. We are not there to scold or discipline. Some of these kids simply needed a bit of focused one-on-one time with somebody who had time "only for them." However, if neither of us was enjoying the time, there wasn't going to be much point in continuing.

I racked my brain to try and come up with ways to engage him, and that's when I remembered how much my own kids used to love colored ink pens. I trotted off to Wal-Mart and bought one green ink pen for him and a box of colored pencils—as backup.

The next week we met, and when it was time to start our word/sentence writing I told him I had something special for him to write with that day, and what would he think about trying to write with green ink instead of that pencil that kept breaking?

HALLELUJAH!—the child's whole demeanor shot up like a skyscraper in Manhattan!

But he was a smart little guy: "Now, I don't want to waste any of my green ink by writing any more than one sentence."

Oy, vey, I thought to myself. Nothing is ever easy.

"Okay," I said, "then how about writing one sentence in green ink, and two more using these new colored pencils I brought?" It worked. He agreed, and he wrote the best three sentences he'd written so far in the time I'd been tutoring him. (You just have to love it when things work out!)

Well, three good sentences calls for something more than just an ordinary drawn-on "star," so out came the red foil stick-on stars I'd brought along that day. He enjoyed pasting those stars on his journal book--where he wanted them. I considered this victory No. 2 for the day.

"I want to take the green pen home with me," he said, when he finished.

"But if you take it home and forget it, we won't have it for next week," I said, praying that he'd be satisfied.

"Well, how about if we just put it in my locker then?"

"But sometimes things can disappear from lockers and then we'd be without a green pen again," I said, trying to coach him past this.

He thought this over.

I thought even quicker.

"How about if I bring the pen back every week with me and at the end of this school year you take it home? It'll be yours for good," I promised him.

We had arrived at an accord!

I didn't know if I could keep him motivated with this green-ink/red-foil-stars thing for another two months or not, but I was determined that I would try.

Sometimes all that's needed is a new trick mixed into the old routine, for any of us—young and old alike.

TABULA RASA (CLEAN SLATE)
By Rosemary McKinley

Innocence personified
This newborn---like all before her
Yet, she is the
Child of my child
A clean slate stands before us

My child was once like her
Now she is a woman
Her new addition sits before us

Let us begin again
To nurture her
To encourage play and
The wonder of life
Every day that she is near
Lest we lose this second chance
To fill the clean slate
With all that is good and
Wonderful with this world

NEW GROWTH
By Mary Elizabeth Laufer

The child found God
not in the stained-glass windows,
not in the smooth wooden pews,
not even in his lessons at Sunday school.

The child found God in a vegetable garden.
His mother placed ten bean seeds in his small hand,
and one at a time he poked them into the soil.
He watered them and waited.

One morning the ground cracked open,
a curled stem bent upward,
two pale green leaves slowly unfolded
and reached for the sun.

As the child watched this miracle,
another seed sprouted in his young soul.
He found God in every new leaf,
every fragile bud, every tender bean.

TO BE A MOM
By Paula Timpson

To be a mom
is to learn how to truly Love~
Forgiveness comes and forgetfulness too,
remembering only the good
that comes our way each day~
Listen in to a child's
laughter~
Promises arrive in Rainbow's pastels~
Life calls us to
surrender to the One
who made the stars shine bright every night
A child leads us to find
Grace,
Hope
Peace and
Joy!

LIFE LESSON, TAKE TWO
By David MacWilliams

My family and I were camping a few summers ago at Mancos State Park in southwestern Colorado. My family includes my wife Pilar, our then seven-year-old son Nick, and our then three-year-old daughter Elena. We had set up our giant Coleman tent under a couple of tall pine trees in a site near the edge of the reservoir where we wanted to go fishing. We weren't too far into the wild. Though beyond electricity and running water, the site was a few hundred yards from a squat, brown, cinder brick outhouse—a pit toilet, one of those monstrous and often stinky things with a heavy metal door and a hard plastic seat set in concrete, with a sign above the seat which read, "Please do not throw trash in the toilet as it is extremely difficult to remove." If you've ever camped in Colorado, you've seen these signs. If you haven't, take it from me: they tell the truth.

Besides our one fishing pole, we had lots of gear, naturally. The most distinctive item among all of it was Elena's hat. She was very proud of it, this floppy, oversized khaki sun hat. She'd gotten it a week earlier from her teacher at the summer bible school she'd attended, a reward for memorizing a short passage from the Bible, and every kid got one, no matter how badly they mangled their assigned verse. Nicholas had one too, but never wore it after the first day; it wasn't cool. Both kids had written their names on the band inside the crown of the hat, and they had decorated their hats with a small selection of brightly colored pins, one which read "God is Love," another which read "Jesus Loves You," and another of the Colorado state flag.

Elena called the hat "My Jesus Hat" because her teacher had told her that it would cover her as if it were the hand of God. Elena wore it all the time, even when she crawled into her sleeping bag at night. On our last night her long hair got entangled in the Jesus Loves You pin, but she didn't care at all. She carefully removed the hat and patiently unwound her hair from the pin, smiling all the while.

We broke camp on a Sunday morning. I struck the tent and laid it out on the ground and disconnected its long poles and piled them at its side, next to our lonely fishing pole, which had not caught a single fish because Nick had irreversibly snarled the line with his second cast the day before. The kids were already climbing into the car, but I asked Pilar if she could take Elena to pee before we got on the road. The two of them walked hand-in-hand to the outhouse through shafts of morning sunlight that bristled against the gold and silver pins on Elena's hat.

I'd just packed the tent into its bag and was poised over the bag's gaping mouth, ready to shove the poles in when I heard Elena screaming in a way I hadn't heard since her early infancy. She had nearly died at birth due to a heart condition; her great arteries were reversed, sort of tangled. Pilar and I were distraught with fear and thought we might lose her, but a very skillful surgeon untangled her arteries when she was only a week old, just when, in his words, she was strong enough to scream loud enough to wake every infant in the neonatal intensive care ward. Even three years later though, a scream from her could still seize me by the throat. I spun round and saw her returning from the pit toilet, bareheaded, bent over nearly double, with fists clenched. "My Jesus hat! My Jesus hat! My Jesus hat!" she shrieked.

"Down the chute?" I asked Pilar.

She shrugged. "Just as I lifted her off the seat it fell in."

We both looked at Elena, who stood howling over the cold ashes of our last night's fire. My wife then looked at me. "Maybe if you take the fishing pole," she said.

"Maybe if *I* take the fishing pole? You want me to fish the thing out?"

"Well," she began.

And I thought to myself. "And just how am I supposed to cast it?"

As if reading my thoughts, Pilar bit her lower lip and added, "Maybe if you take the tent pole and stick a hook to the end with duct tape."

Duct tape: Pilar's answer to all of life's ills. Wanna fix a broken window? Duct tape. Gotta fix a bike's flat tire? Duct tape. Bleeding? Duct tape. "Pilar," I asked, "and if I tape a hook to the end, just what bait do you think the hat will bite?"

"Then maybe you can spear it," she replied.

I had an imaginary glimpse of myself standing in the outhouse door with a fifteen foot tent pole aloft in my hands, one foot braced against the rim of the toilet, like Captain Ahab with his foot on the prow of the whaling boat, me, trying to harpoon a Jesus hat with a spinner taped to the end. And I pictured Ranger Rick walking up behind me, in his broad brimmed ranger hat shaking his head and with his hands on his hips, already imagining himself at his dinner table that evening telling his wife, "Honey, you won't believe what I saw today."

I shoved the poles into the bag. "Pilar," I said, "Maybe it's time that Elena learned a lesson about loss."

This lesson really was not easy for either of us because Elena would've died but for the skill of her surgeon three years earlier. He unraveled her arteries and gave us back our newborn daughter. Afterwards he warned us that we could expect one side effect from the heart condition and surgery: that we would spoil her rotten for the rest of her childhood. There was one more he hadn't mentioned, however, and it was even more powerful: that we could never bear to see her heart broken again. Such had indeed been the case so far — but that would not be the case on this day.

Elena cried and whined at intervals during the three-hour trip home. Her determination to will the hat back out of the toilet was truly awe inspiring. We stopped at a convenience store along the way where a kindly, grandmotherly sort took an interest in Elena's pain and suggested that we buy her another hat. "Look at all the pretty hats on this rack," the kindly lady said pointing to the display near the cash register. "I want MY Jesus hat," Elena growled. The poor lady's eyes widened.

That evening, I was putting our gear away in a hall closet where I keep the camping equipment. Elena was behind me, watching, sulking. Now that I was putting the stuff away for good, she must have realized that there was no going back to the pit, no retrieving the hat. Bereft of hope, she stood there with her shoulders slumped and her expression vacant. I paused a moment and just watched her. I felt sorry for her and tried to console myself. Lesson learned, I thought. All a part of growing up. I had nothing to say to her, however, so I turned and started pushing the tent bag onto the top shelf. Then it happened. The fit was tight, so I pulled the bag out to try again, when the Jesus hat, *the* Jesus hat, tumbled out of the closet, brushed past my face, and landed at Elena's feet upside down.

The band inside the crown faced us and clearly read E-L-E-N-A.

Elena shouted, "My Jesus hat!" She scooped it up in ecstasy, embraced it, and put it back on her head, then tore down the hall to the living room to show her mom the incredible discovery, bracing the hat to her head with two hands lest it should fall again. It hadn't returned, of course. She'd been wearing her brother's hat by mistake the entire camping trip, and it was *his* hat that had fallen down irretrievably into the pit, but not, as far as Elena knew, beyond the reach of the miraculous.

And so she learned a second lesson about loss, something her mom and I had learned at her birth. Sometimes you get things back, and when you do, you hold on with both hands.

MOTHER AND CHILD
By Jean L. Kaess

In a dim room,
Wrapped in a huge squishy blanket,
Christmas lights twinkle softly
As I hum Silent Night.
You sigh, your stomach satiated for three more hours.
I sigh, my Soul satiated.

Our hearts sync into one soft rhythm,
Slowly beating out our messages to each other.
Swaddled in my arms,
You discover tender midnight in wonder.
I drift in wonder
Of milky baby breath
And sweet newborn hair
While we rock
In soothing, subtle sway.

The tree, our only companion this cold December night,
Keeps vigil as you sleep in Heavenly Peace.

JOY IN THE WORLD
By Don Segal

Her face brightened
With her hands full of,
That Baby!

Heart full of sad
Replaced by a moment of,
That Baby!

She laughed as
Her glasses came off,
Finger poking her ear.

Baby, not knowing anything,
Took her out of her depth.

HAIR FOR G-MA
By Francine L. Baldwin-Billingslea

We love our children, but there is something so special about the love you have for your grandchildren. It was a different kind of love. It's the kind that allows them to get away with stuff that you never allowed your own children to get away with. It's the kind that makes you stick up for them when you know they should get time-out for the rest of their lives, but you just can't find it in your heart to tell their parents the wrongs they've done because you want to spare the harsh discipline you know their parents will give, and they rightfully deserve. It's also the kind of love that makes your grandchildren run to you and it's the kind that will make them do the unthinkable to make you happy as my grandkids did for me.

At the age of four, Aaron, the eldest of my two grandsons became obsessed with Superman, Batman and every other superhero with a cape. As soon as he opened his eyes in the morning, he'd reach over and grab his pillowcase, I mean his cape that was made out of an old pillow case, (God-forbid if he heard you calling his cape a pillowcase), and he'd fly to the bathroom, then into the kitchen to eat his breakfast. He'd run around the house all day, arms stretched out, fighting crime, saving and helping all of those in need in his imaginary world.

Aaron thought he could do everything his superheroes could do and it's not as if he didn't try. One day while we were watching television, something came on about starving babies in a third world country, he watched with undivided attention, all of a sudden, he jumped up and ran into the kitchen and got potato chips, juice sips and cookies and came running, I mean flying to the front door and tried to open it. I said, "Hey young man, what are you doing and where do you think you're going?" Full of excitement he said, "G-ma, I've gotta give those kids some food!" Needless to say, we began to watch his every flight closer than ever.

At the age of six, Aaron was still flying around trying to save the world with his five-year-old brother Jalani now imitating and following his every move. During this time, I was diagnosed with breast cancer, and after the second chemotherapy treatment I began to lose my hair. Feeling quite depressed and anxious, hoping it would lift my spirits, I went to spend a few weeks with my daughter and grandchildren. One evening my grandsons came into the room and asked what happened to my hair. While trying to explain the situation to them, I started crying. Jalani climbed into my lap, hugged me and said, "Don't cry G-ma, Aaron can get you some hair, he can do everything!" I looked over at Aaron who was standing there with tears in his eyes. Not wanting the boys to be upset or see me so distraught, I put a smile on my face and told them not to worry and with their help, I was going to be just fine. I then told them I was going to take my medicine and go to bed and I'll see them in the morning. We hugged and said our good-nights. Aaron put his arm around his little brother's shoulder and I laughed as they turned and slowly walked out of the room with their dirty, wrinkled, stinky capes dragging behind them. I took my medication along with a prescription sleep aide and called it a night.

Sounds of my daughter yelling and the four kids crying woke me. Drowsy, I looked at the clock, it was 8 am. I couldn't imagine what all the commotion was about. I rolled over and tried to go back to sleep. In-between dozing off and on, I heard my daughter asking or rather yelling, "You did what? Why? You both know better! Oh, my God!" I heard my four-year-old granddaughter Zariah crying and screaming at her brothers, and my ten-year-old granddaughter Zoë was chiming in with her. From what I could hear and understand, the boys were in serious trouble and the girls, along with my daughter, were flaming mad at them. I wondered what they could've done to get the girls so mad and since I couldn't go back to sleep, I decided to get up and go to my little buddies' rescue.

I sat on the edge of the bed and found that I was still quite groggy from the medication. I squinted and wondered what in the world was all over my bed, it looked like little strands of hair, but I knew that couldn't be. I went into the kitchen and before I could say anything, my daughter and granddaughters abruptly stopped fussing, looked and busted out laughing. They were laughing so hard, they were bent over, holding their stomachs. They could hardly talk as they pointed and kept trying to tell me to go and look in the mirror. When I went to look, I was horrified! I had patches and pieces of different colored hair with dry, peeling, white stuff all over the front of my forehead and down one side of my head. I laughed and cried all at the same time as I found out that the boys had cut all the hair off of Zoë and Zariah's dolls and had used Elmer's glue to try and paste it on my bald head while I was sleeping.

I truly believe that was the real beginning of my recovery. They say that laughter is like a medicine, and every time I felt down physically, mentally or emotionally, I'd think about what my grandsons did for me and I would laugh so hard, that I instantaneously felt better. Many times it was just for that moment, but I knew the thought of their mischievous attentiveness would bring me a feeling of exuberance that would last for the rest of my life.

When my granddaughters realized why the boys cut their dolls hair off, they reluctantly forgave their brothers and later told me that they would've helped them.

I'll always remember the times I sat in the chemo room, or laid in my hospital bed telling that story and hearing the laughter or seeing the smiles from the doctors and nurses, but most importantly, from the other patients. Laughter is contagious, effective and definitely has healing powers.

Yes, I wanted to live, and when I saw the love and concern that my grandchildren had for me, I knew that I had to live, and my undying love for them gave me such a burning desire, that I knew that I was going to live.

That was a little more than ten years ago and it's still a belly buster. I know we'll laugh about that for the rest of our lives. That was the best, the sincerest and the most benevolent thing anybody could have ever done for me during that critical time in my life and because of that, my grandsons will always be my heroes.

My oldest granddaughter Zoë, is presently in the United States Air Force and when she came home this year for the holidays, she brought that topic up, after we all had a good laugh, I said, "Zoë, I can't believe you still remember that." She said, "G-Ma, we'll always remember that!" Then she got up and hugged me and the other kids joined in yelling, "Group hug!" A grandmother's love allowed my arms to stretch around all four as they towered over me and I tearfully whispered, "I love you." "We love you too G-Ma came the reply," and then my heroes yelled, "Okay, can we eat now?" I laughed as I said, "Of course you can, let's set the table." The girls immediately went to work as the boys sat back down in front of the television. The girls fussed with them as usual, the boys ignored them as usual, my daughter yelled at them as usual, and I smiled as usual as I thought, there's nothing like grandchildren, no matter how big or small or how young or old, and I felt thankful that I was healed and they were now old enough that I could sleep safely around them.

Previously published in *Through it all and out on the other side (Xlibris)*

SHEEP-LESSNESS
By Cona F. Gregory-Adams

Never a dull moment, with small fry in tow,
expressing opinions as they learn and grow.

Imaginations always working overtime,
throwing out questions that boggle the mind.

"Mom, I can't sleep," the little girl announces.
Mother advised counting sheep, jumping fences.

Soon, a small excited voice cries out in wonder,
"Mom, it's not working, they're squeezing under!"

SHINE THE LIGHT
By Tina Traster

I heard her calling "Mommy, Mommy" before I opened the door. She tore off the school bus as though it were on fire.

"I tried out for solo, I tried out for solo," she squealed, pushing open the door. "I'm going to get it this time. Mrs. Anderson said I was great!"

"I think you're going to get it, too," I said.

"Listen to this, Mommy," she said, still wearing her winter jacket and hat and over-stuffed purple backpack. She spread her feet apart, took a breath, and belted out "Shine the Light, Shine The Light..." with Gospel-singer force.

"Wow, Julia," I said, amazed at my nine-year-old. "You really deserve the solo this year."

"Thanks, Mom," she said, peeling off her coat.

Six years earlier, when Julia was in nursery school, she could not learn lyrics or hand movements.

Year-end winter concerts caused unspeakable dread in our household. It bothered me more than it did my husband Rick. It was painful to watch our daughter on stage, participating but not really there. No one thought she had a learning disability, because she didn't. Nursery school teachers didn't understand why Julia had trouble being part of a group. They didn't know why she hid under a desk or kept to herself. They didn't know she'd been behaving like this since we'd adopted her from Siberia when she was eight months old. They didn't know because we didn't tell them.

The nursery school folks were doing their best to "manage" her, as were we. Rick and I convinced ourselves she'd come around, she'd become "normal." We hoped and prayed she'd find her way into the fabric of her family, her community. I tried not to think about the implications of a baby starting her life as one in ten in a sterile little room in a Siberian orphanage. I'd push away the memory of seeing her in that crib, a brown tea concoction in a bottle at her lips, swaddled so tightly she couldn't fuss. This way the caretakers could attend to all the babies.

Because we took her home at eight months, I figured we'd love her to pieces and erase early damage.

I didn't want to believe I could be wrong. But after Julia's year-end concert at nursery school, I broke down. She was disruptive on stage. Jocelyn pulled her off after the first song and held her in her lap. I cried, hoping no one would notice.

Then Rick and I got busy. It was time to learn about Reactive Attachment Disorder – a syndrome I was vaguely familiar with but didn't want to believe had anything to do with my child. Julia was the textbook case – she exhibited a host of behaviors associated with foreign adoptees who have difficulty attaching when they are brought home. Academics say early, painful separation from a birth mother causes trauma. The child internalizes the belief she can rely on no one other than herself. Along the way she learns crying is pointless, the world is not a nurturing place. Children like this endlessly seek attention but they're never sated. What we saw in Julia was a child who was always trying to control her world – and others in it. She had trouble relaxing into an embrace. I remember the days when she was in her stroller. She viewed it as confinement; she could never sit back and enjoy the ride.

The more we read, the more we understood Julia. Now it made sense why she recoiled when she was held, that she hardly cried and when she did it was always brief. Why she never chose a favorite teddy.

After many long nights of conversation, Rick and I decided to undertake "Operation Love." We were hell-bent on bringing Julia back from the abyss. We felt we had a good understanding of the problem and between us, we believed if we worked with her, we stood a chance of rescuing her from a life of isolation. It was – and remains – a daily effort. It is unnatural for a child to be so resistant to love. We found ourselves saying things like "I know it's scary to love your Mommy and Daddy, but it's okay. They love you and they always will."

We also figured out that Julia found relief in the refuge of punishment. A time-out for a normal kid might be a hardship; or at least a time to contemplate bad behavior. For Julia, it was a relief and a chance to re-charge her batteries; to retreat and later create more chaos. Chaos, we learned, is the weapon of the child who suffers from Reactive Attachment Disorder. We learned how to counter its weight by underplaying our reactions to her.

Over the years, we learned to live with patience, disappointment, and poignant victories. Perhaps that's any parent's story. But holiday concerts remained a challenge. By first and second grades, we'd begun to offer rewards – "if you do a good job at the holiday concert, you'll get a present." Indeed, the prospect of a new Lego set worked somewhat.

On a late December day, when Julia was in third grade, I asked her how the holiday concert songs were going. She shrugged.

"Let me see the lyrics," I said.

She thumbed through her messy folder.

"I don't have them," she said.

"Well, can you sing them?"

She didn't know a word. The concert was a week away. Dread encased me.

I got hold of the music teacher the next day to get the lyrics. I worked with Julia tirelessly day and night to make sure she knew every word. We fought all the way through. The night of the concert, I left my seat in mid-auditorium and sat at the foot of the stage. Julia waved at me nervously. Then the music began and she shot me a quick smile. She sang every word. She belonged.

Afterward she asked for a present.

I said "We have a big hug and we are very proud."

She seemed okay with that.

I admit I was surprised when six months later, for the June concert, Julia announced her intention to try out for a solo. At every concert, six kids sing a couple of lines in one of three songs. Every night I heard her rehearsing in her bedroom.

"She really, really wants that solo," I said to Rick, gauging his reaction.

He gave me one of his long gazes and said, "I'm going to write to Mrs. Anderson."

"Do you think that's a good idea?" I asked.

"Just something gentle to say Julia's been working really hard and she'd love to be picked for a solo."

I half-wished we could explain the whole thing to Mrs. Anderson. To tell her what a long and hard road it has been to get Julia engaged in her life. I gave Mrs. Anderson the benefit of the doubt. She must see how far Julia's come, I thought, hopefully.

Julia was not picked for the solo.

In a follow-up email, Mrs. Anderson told my husband she didn't think Julia was serious enough about wanting the solo.

A few weeks later, Julia left for a sleep-away camp that specializes in theater and performance. On visiting day we watched her do a solo magic act, dance in a musical and recite lines. In this magical place in the Catskill Mountains, Julia had learned the joy of being part of something; she learned it's okay to trust others and to have others trust you.

When we picked her up in August, she chattered incessantly about camp and her friends and the shows she was in. Out of nowhere she said, "I'm going to try out for solo again this year, Mommy." She was talking about her fourth-grade winter concert in August!

She made good on her declaration. For two weeks in early

December she practiced "Shine the Light." She was sure she'd get it this year. She was called back twice. But on the day before the concert – a day after she'd skipped down the path to tell me how good her tryout went – she was crushed.

I opened the front door and she collapsed into tears. Through gasping breaths she said she didn't get it.

"And you know what else?" she asked.

"What?" I said.

"Mrs. Anderson came to get me and a couple of other kids for the final tryout and in front of them she said to me, 'Now don't have your Mommy and Daddy call me if you don't get the solo.'"

You know those moments in life when you feel as though you could wring someone's neck with your bare hands?

I had Julia repeat the story twice just to make sure I heard it right and to check that she was telling the truth.

Then I said, "If you want to boycott the concert, that is fine with me."

She looked at me quizzically, as if to say, "Why does that work? How does that make you feel better?" I was too busy muttering with anger to explain. I called Rick. He said he'd arrange a meeting with the principal because he viewed Mrs. Anderson's words as abusive.

When I kissed Julia good-night, I said, "Forget about the solo. It's not important. And remember, you can boycott if you want."

The next morning Julia tore down the steps yelling, "Daddy, where's the white shirt you ironed for me? I need it for tonight's concert."

Julia looked big on the stage that night. She knew the words cold. She was somewhat forlorn afterward, still smarting over not being given the solo.

"You don't have to tryout for solo in June," I said, on the ride back home.

"I'm not going to," she said. "Never again."

The next day my husband and I met with the principal and Mrs. Anderson. Mrs. Anderson half-admitted she'd said something about "not telling your parents to call me if you don't get the solo" but she watered down the story and pretended she'd said it to several children. We knew Julia's version was truthful.

More importantly than admonishing Mrs. Anderson for her inappropriate remark, I told her how defeated Julia felt and I thought it was a shame she couldn't see how far Julia had come. The discussion got heated but in fleeting moments I actually felt sorry for Mrs. Anderson because behind her bravado and defensiveness, I suspected this teacher, this woman with bad teeth and nervous gestures, may have once been an outsider herself.

Mrs. Anderson agreed to meet with Julia and apologize.

That afternoon, Julia bounded down our path with her usual verve.

"Anything unusual happen this afternoon?" I asked.

"How do you know?" she said.

"I don't know," I said. "What happened?"

"Mrs. Anderson said she was sorry and she said I should keep trying," she said.

"Okay, but you don't have to," I said.

"I know, but I'm going to," she said. "I'm going to keep trying until I get it."

Previously published at Mothering .com

NEWBORN
By Louise Webster

A blanketed warmth that nestles
Beside my beating heart
Sweet essence of heaven's newborn scent
Tiny features mirror cupid's art
Mewing coos, a tender cry
In my own arms
The gift of life

ERIN'S BUSY DAY
 (AT AGE 2)
By Susan Mahan

She likes to climb inside her fort
or perch above her slide.
She peeks out from behind a book.
She loves a basket ride.

She might go down the basement
and crawl through Wonderland.
She gobbles up her oatmeal
and thinks that cheese is grand.

She likes to browse through catalogs
to order Daddy shoes.
She reads the paper, page by page
to keep up with the news.

She schedules time for crosswords,
loves videos on Pooh,
She listens to her music
and will make some tea for you.

She loves to go to playgrounds
to swing on monkey bars.
She gazes out her window
at Mister Moon and stars.

And when it's time to go to sleep,
when everything's been done,
she tells her puppy and blankie
that it's time to end the fun.

Love, Nana

COMPROMISING JOY
By Jane Blanchard

My daughter, how alike we are in mind
And manner, speech and gesture, form and face.
When God surveyed all time and womankind,
He measured me in His abounding grace
And marked my nascent womb, my life, my hopes
With seven pounds of compromising joy.
Look at you now! A five-year old who copes
So well alone, a minx who seems to toy
With my desires as well as my affection
And only offers love upon caprice.
It's true I often make you a projection
Of my person. Yet when I won't release
Yourself from mine, your protest says it all:
"But, Mama, you are big, and I am small."

Previously published in *Assisi* (Fall 2011/Spring 2012)

THE GLORIOUS MORNING OF THE DANCING PONYTAIL
By Scott Peterson

My daughter is on her way to kindergarten early enough in the fall that her hair is still streaked blond by the summer sun and a parade of freckles marches across her nose and splashes over her rosy cheeks. Her hair is pulled back in a high, tight ponytail that dances and wiggles every time she moves, as if wired directly to her brain and every emotion, every quiver of excitement is broadcasted straight through her ponytail out to the rest of the world. She carries a backpack that gives her the humped look of a turtle, and inside are all the earthly possessions she needs to get through the school day; the new set of markers still bright and sharp and not mushed into nothingness by over-eager hands; the almost new notebook I brought back for her from a conference at Michigan State University; a favorite book she just has to share with her teacher; and the chubby little bear that gets her through the long, lonely bus journey when she can't sit next to her best friend.

She walks down the driveway and joins the gaggle of neighborhood kids on their way to the bus stop. At first she mingles with the group as they amble up the road, but then, no longer able to contain her kindergarten excitement, her feet shift into a trot. Just as she breaks free from the crowd, a ray of early morning sun slants over the embankment across the street and hits her ponytail, transforming it into a beacon of dancing yellow light. The scene takes my breath away, and I stand and watch until the dancing ponytail disappears inside the bus and roars off to school, even though I have pressing business at work and will now have to fight the rush hour traffic. This moment is a rare and precious gift, a privileged glimpse into a world all most too good to be true.

And maybe it is. This perfect hasp of light and air and innocence is indeed a powerful mix, but a fragile one as well. The unchallenged belief that each and every morning will be as bright and shiny as this one is an impossible standard to maintain, beyond even the best of educational institutions to meet. The daily grind of homework and endless high stakes testing, the intense and often brutal buffeting from peers, the gritty reality of everyday life will soon enough begin to rub the glow off my daughter's light and tarnish her youthful optimism.

As the bus chugs away, I realize that I have learned something about my role as a father. My biggest tasks aren't going to be teaching my daughter how to read or ride a bike or pitch a decent fastball. My real job is to keep that light glowing when everybody and everything seems hell bent on putting it out. Today, on this glorious morning of the dancing ponytail, her vision is so lofty as to be beyond reach. To carry around such expectations is an almost unbearable burden, a prescription for disappointment. My job will be to help her learn to deal with life as it comes, not as it should be. I will have to learn how to sift through all that is tossed her way and to pick the important things. As Martin Barrett writes in his fine essay, *Climbing Toward Christmas*, "The miracle is not something that happens to you - it is all around you, you are embedded in it, moving through it, part of it." My task is to help her realize that life is rich and deep and full of joy, and our job is to identify those miracles no matter how they come wrapped.

I learned one other important thing on this glorious morning of the dancing ponytail, something about the love between a parent and child. Before today, I thought it was a warm and cuddly thing, like the smell of baby powder and shampoo after an evening bath, or brushing the hair out of my daughter's eyes as I read her a bedtime story or rocking a spooked child back to sleep after a bad dream. It is all these things, of course, but also something much deeper and more complicated. What is unleashed in the soul between a parent and a child is a wild thing, sharp and edgy as well as soft and warm. Love is a multi-faceted emotion, with pain and tears, endless worry and sleepless nights as much a part of the mix as light and glory. I will have to pick my way carefully through this complicated maze of emotions, but if I watch my step, listen and learn as I go along, and do my job well, then maybe I can help to keep the glorious light of the dancing ponytail glowing.

DUTY
From a single mother to her son
By Roshanda Johnson

I know you're tired of my speeches,
but what kind of mama would I be
if I didn't try to reach you?
I know there are things
only a man can teach you,
but he's not here,
and even when he was
he made one thing clear-
He wasn't interested in being a father.

He wanted to be your partner,
your homie,
your ace.
I'm not knocking your bond with him,
but God gave me you to raise.
You are not just my son.
You are my duty.
If I do nothing else in life with honors
I raise you with a purple heart
that beats despite the bruising.

I cannot be the man you want me to be.
I can only be that which I am.
If you feel I've been too hard on you,
it's true.
It's tough molding a man
with a woman's hands.
I'm doing all that I can
to make up for him being less than a man.

Son, you don't get it now,
but one day you'll understand

that whether or not he comes on Saturday
you still have to eat
throughout the work week.
Whether or not his check hits the bank
you still have to have shoes on your feet.
He may teach you about the birds and bees,
may even make it to every football game,
but I gave you a home in my womb
and the breath that I breathe
before your daddy even knew your first name.

And I'll keep giving
as long as I'm living;
Beyond his 48 hours
to my twenty thousand, one hundred sixty minutes.
My love is infinite.
It can extinguish
all the hell you raise.
Especially on those days
when you blame me for the mistakes he made.
I take it like a soldier.
Never waging war against him
'cause when you get older
you will see
that this lifelong battle you've been fighting
hasn't really been about me.

It hasn't been about the trash,
Or expecting **As** in your class.
It hasn't been about my so-called stupid rules
or popping up at your school.
It hasn't been about work,
or making you tuck in your shirt for church.
This lifelong battle has been about your hurt.

Let me share your sorrow.
It's been so many years since he dropped that bomb,
yet the vapors of unsullied pain
remain as fresh as a blooming tomorrow.
You can't stop to smell my roses
for sniffing at his weeds.
Know this my Son,
to him you may only be a seed,
but to me

you are the cultivation of all God believed
when HE said,
Let us make man…
And it's hard work
being a single mother
trying to carry out the Master's plan.
You don't have to get it now,
but one day you'll understand.

You are not just my son.
You are my duty.
And if I do nothing else in life with honors
I raise you with a purple heart
that beats despite the bruising.

DREAMLAND
By Lynn C. Johnston

As I watch you sleeping
I pray sweet dreams fill your head
And your heart soars high on angels' wings
As you lie quietly in bed

May you drift off to a land
Full of enchantment and delight
Where every rainbow has a pot of gold
Glistening in the bright sunlight

A place where heroes never stumble
Riding bravely on white steeds
And nothing is impossible
As long as you believe

But should a ghost or demon
Ever disturb your peaceful sleep
Know that I'll be by your side
To slay it at your feet

Then I'll hold you close
And rock you gently in my arms
Until you're safely back in Dreamland
With all its magic and its charms

Previously published in Angel's Dance:
A Collection of Uplifting & Inspirational Poetry (Whispering Angel Books)

ANGELS NEED US, TOO
By Barbara Kay Daniel

My son asked me to come to California for a year. He wanted me to be full-time caretaker for my ten-month-old granddaughter, Adele, when her mother returned to work. Elated, I put my life on hold in rural Virginia to brave the Los Angeles fast pace. Several months into my stay, something happened which made me realize there was an even greater reason why I was needed out there.

Every day, I took Adele to the South Gardner kiddy playground. For some reason, we went earlier than usual that morning. This play area isn't fenced in; it's just off the large parking lot of a senior recreation center. The parking lot abuts Pan Pacific Park. This part of the massive park is wooded and more isolated. On the other side of Pan Pacific is "The Grove," a famous shopping mall. Foreigners, vacationers, and locals crowd there to ride the trolley and shop expensive stores. It was the perfect setup for a child kidnapping.

The play area was full of young mothers and a few nannies. Adele slid down all the low slides, and played in the sandbox with the other toddlers. It wasn't long before she was ready for her snack and morning nap. I had strapped her into her stroller and started home, when something told me to turn back around.

I looked at all of the mothers and nannies talking to each other in animated conversations. Suddenly, I realized that I was the only one who saw a little boy leave the sandbox, and run across the parking lot after an elderly couple. He must have thought they were his grandparents. They didn't notice him and got in their car.

The toddler took off again, running straight toward the woods. I felt such a fear descend on my heart. Something told me if he got into that park, he would be kidnapped or found too late. I couldn't leave Adele to run after him, so I did the next best thing.

"Who's missing their little blond-haired boy?!" I screamed in feral panic, waving my arm in the direction of the running child. "Hurry! He's already across the parking lot, headed for the woods!"

They all looked at me like I was crazy, but stopped talking. At least I had their attention.

"Somebody had better get him! He left the sandbox only a second ago!" I yelled in disbelief. A young mother looked around. She jumped to her feet, when she didn't see her child anywhere. "That way!" I cried. "Hurry!"

She reached him just as his little head bobbed out of sight. I waited until she brought her precious child safely back to the sandbox; only then did I feel okay to leave.

All the way home to my son's apartment, chills rippled over my entire body with thrills of joy. It was like I had momentarily slipped into a M. Night Shyamalan world, where a too-perfect coincidence is proof that a Higher Power arranged it. Could it possibly have been just a coincidence that a woman had to travel all the way across country to save one child's life? I am grateful I heard the silent call of his guardian angel, and turned back around. I pray the Higher Power will always make sure somebody is there, looking out for my little Adele.

For me, children are God's special gifts; and they all belong to all of us as one great big family.

MY CHILDREN
By Thanecha Senat

My womb has bore no children
However my heart has been filled to capacity
With love that overflows
Love that only children can bring
My children brings me eternal laughter and joy
The beauty of my girls
The rugged playfulness of my boys
My children fill my world with smiles
Their love eases the soul and nourishes the mind

My womb has bore no children
Yet, I cannot live without them
Cannot live without the love that emits from their every breath
Their very life
A love so deep that it cannot be defined nor characterized

MY DAUGHTER
By Holly Day

angel
she rolls over and sighs in her sleep
such a tiny, slight sound
but it fills my whole head.
a song of distant cherubs
the sound of the sun rising.

she
reaches for me in the
dark, chubby hands
instinctively
grappling out in search of my older
worn palms, fingers that feel
purposeless without

her. when did this happen
this point in my life
where all I
ever wanted was
to have her?

CHILDREN POUR LEMONADE INTO THE GULF OF MEXICO
By Sandra Ervin Adams

They cried the night they saw dying pelicans on TV.
In bed after saying prayers,
their little minds contrived a way to help.

The next day their little hands rolled lemons,
combined sour juice
with water
and sugar,
in an attempt to make a desirable drink.

They poured the mixture from a plastic pitcher,
sold it by the cupful,
told reporters of plans
to send their profits to coastal groups
benefiting birds, turtles, fish, and other sea creatures.

Youthful entrepreneurs, yes, but more so,
budding empaths who would grow
to be like their predecessors
several generations ago
who sold flowers
on street corners.

Previously published online at *New Verse News* on June 29, 2010.

BUTTERFLY
By Bridget McNamara-Fenesy

The water hit my face like an icy slap, but by the time my feet followed into the pool it had already begun to feel good. This was the kind of dip I loved – warm summer day, no agenda but relaxing on our first day of vacation. Devon was already in the pool, doing laps.

"Race me, Mom!" she hollered. This was not much of a challenge. She had been swimming competitively since first grade, and was amazing to watch. Her body seemed to skim the water, offering no resistance and gliding as if riding a wave. She loved to beat me, and while her sprints gave me a little exercise, they left me with even less dignity. Maybe, though, I was getting a little bit faster.

"What stroke?" I asked. Didn't really matter – she could beat me at all of them.

"Butterfly!"

"Honey, you know I can't do it – let's do back stroke."

"Today's the day, Mom – I'm gonna teach you" – I had seen that look before. She was not going to take no for an answer. Even at the age of 11, she was determined, and I had learned to pick my battles with her. What the heck – we had nothing else we had to do that day. "Okay, but we're not racing – you have to really teach me," I replied.

"Okay, Mom. No problem," Devon said as she grabbed a paddle board from the side of the pool. "First, we have to get the footwork down. You're going to hold this paddle, and I'll show you what to do with your feet." She jumped out of the pool and came back with what looked like a giant rubber band out of her swim bag. "Put this around your ankles."

I struggled to get the band over my feet as she went on. "Okay, you're a mermaid. You do NOT have two feet - only one fin. Your feet have to stay together. Like this..."

I watched as she effortlessly slid through the water, undulating her legs as if there were no joints, with her feet perfectly connected. They slapped the water in a way that brought to mind a sea otter playing in the surf. Before I knew it, she was on the other side of the pool. "Now your turn!" she yelled from the far wall.

It was nearly impossible to mimic the stroke holding the paddle board, as it kept me afloat. I let go of the board, and immediately felt myself sinking, scrambling to resurface with a clunky rubber band holding my feet together. I choked on a gulp full of water.

"Mom, stand up! You're at the shallow end of the pool," Devon laughed. I realized how ridiculous I looked, as my feet touched down on secure concrete.

"Let me catch my breath," I said. I tried again. This time, knowing I could touch down, it was easier. My feet smacked awkwardly, and they pushed to come apart, but the band did its job. I started to feel it. Still herky-jerky, but my ankles held as I tried to hold the image of a mermaid gliding toward Poseiden. By the time I reached Devon, my quads burned.

"Good, Mom, good. A little bit more like a platypus than a mermaid, but you're getting there," she giggled. "Do three laps like that, and if you slide into a groove, we can move on to the arms." I didn't have the heart to tell her that three more laps would likely put me into cardiac arrest. After one lap, she hollered that I should take the band off, but pretend it was still there. Removing the band felt like I had taken an anchor off my legs, and while my footwork got a little bit sloppy, it was far less tiring without the restraints.

"You're doing great, Mom," she encouraged. "Let's move on to the arms. Okay, your arms are going to lift you right out of the water. This time, pretend you're a dolphin. You're underwater, and see something at the surface. Burst to the surface, and lift yourself up and out. Crown of your head to the sky, face to the water. Let's see what you got." I could hear her swim coach channeled through her instructions. Nice to know she was paying attention. I smiled as I slid underwater.

I tried with no success. My upper body felt like lead. I could not heave myself above the surface. I was thankful the water was cool, as by now I would've been soaked with sweat if I'd been in the gym. My shoulders ached. "I'm too heavy!" I called.

"No, Mom, you're not. Use your arms. They are a big giant ice cream scoop. Give me some ice cream scoops!" I heard her yelling "Scoop! Scoop!" each time I tried to surface. My legs had gone to hell, but I was starting to pull a little bit out of the water.

I stopped at her end of the pool, exhausted. She was doubled over in laughter. "Mom, I said ice cream scoop! What kind of scoop are you going for? I want a big, Ben and Jerry's, banana-split size ice cream scoop. You're giving me ice cream slivers like Grandma Fenesy would serve. No good. Big is what we want. Big!"

The image of Grandma Fenesy serving up her notoriously stingy ice cream servings caused me to break a smile through my heaving chest. "That bad, huh?"

"Come on, Mom – you can do it. Race you!" Devon was off.

I spurted and splashed and laughed and slapped my way to the other end of the pool. I was a mermaid serving giant scoops of ice cream. Chocolate and strawberry and vanilla ice cream scoops. I made a mess of my oceanic kitchen, but I made it to the other end of the pool. Devon was waiting with a big wet slimy hug. "You did it Mom – you did the butterfly!"

And I saw the same glint of pride in her eye at my accomplishment that I had felt so many times in the past when she had mastered something she was sure she could not do.

"Thanks, honey – you're a great teacher," I said. And I meant it, as I slid under the surface to glide toward the other end of the pool, with Devon two strokes ahead of me.

CHILD OF MY CHILD
By Rosemary McKinley

Those tiny fingers entwine one of mine
While she sits snugly in the crook
Of my arm
Feeling safe and secure

I know this
By the look in her eyes
As she beseeches mine
And locks them in
I am a grandparent

HAND TO HEART
By Carolyn T. Johnson

In your soulful, blue eyes
I see a divine miracle
wrapped in a strong-willed,
gentle, shy little
bundle of energy
bursting with love
for her new family,
Papa and *her boys*.

I promise to nurture you
like a perfect little daisy
in our garden of love
as you grow and flourish
from a precious child
into a beautiful woman
full of compassion,
charm, intelligence
and faith.

And deliver you
from God's hands
to my heart,
my daughter
Emma.

ABBY EXPLAINS BUS RIDING RULES
TO CARTER ON HIS FIRST FIELD TRIP
By James Bettendorf

Twenty-six toddlers wait in line two by two
for the yellow school bus to take them,
their teachers and chaperones,
to story time at the new library on Nicollet Ave.

> *sit with your field trip buddy*
> *keep bottoms flat on the seat*
> *don't distract the bus driver*
> *no kicking the back of the seat in front of you*

Sitting with the grandkids, I watch out the windows,
wave to truck drivers. Abby is fascinated
by the story of the deer I saw this morning, Carter,
more interested in the backhoe digging on Third Street.

> *be quiet, inside voices*
> *don't fight, teachers will get mad*
> *hands and fingers stay inside the window*
> *ask a parent or teacher for help*

Drips from our boots form dirty little lakes
on the bus floor, hats and coats become undone.
Oohs and aahs when we bounce through a pothole,
giggles when there is a splash.

> *save your questions until we get off the bus*
> *walking feet, no running*
> *eat all your snack before you get back on the bus*
> *be sure to thank the driver*

One child writes MOM on the frosted window.
It reads the same whether you're safe
inside the bus, or in that distant city
on the other side of the window.

LIAR, LIAR, PANTS ON FIRE
By N. K. Weddle

I buckle my four-year-old grandson into his king seat in the back of my car. He is happy and ready for a day of fun. Playing with his superhero toy, he tells me, "Let's go, Joe. My grandma always says that. She's funny! Do you know my grandma?"

Children have an innocent way of putting adults in the most uncomfortable position. How can I explain to a four-year-old that his grandma and I once loved one another madly? How can I explain that for twenty years we shared a home, a life, a thousand dreams, but now, we no longer speak to each other or about each other? The birth of our children, the nights of holding one another, all the promises made are now promises broken. That explanation would be complex. I can imagine his retort: *Liar, liar, pants on fire.* I manage a weak: "We have met."

Holding his superhero above his head, my grandson makes swooshing sounds as the superhero flies to and fro racing to some imaginary rescue. Superhero suddenly stops flying. My grandson's face becomes thoughtful. "Grandma is grandma and you are grandpa." The wheels and gears of his four-year-old mind are working. "You and Grandma have almost the same name." That said, the superhero swooshes once more to the rescue.

My little man, sitting high in his king seat, buckled in for safety, is secure and content while driving a spike of aching regret into my consciousness. He is pouring salt into an unhealed wound. Is the painful 'we don't love each other anymore, but we both love you' speech coming? I don't want to repeat the speech my ex-wife and I gave to our children years ago. Will I see the lost look I once saw in my children's eyes reflected in my grandson's eyes as I try to explain what I don't understand myself?

I try to distract him by changing the subject. "I'm hungry. What do you say we go get a hamburger?"

My grandson's face lights up with the thought of a hamburger. "Let go to Grandma's. She makes the best hamburgers."

I turn from my position in the driver's seat so I can face him.

Resting my chin on my hand, I steel myself to give him the 'we love you…but' speech. Before I can start my spiel, my little man states out of the blue: "I love my grandma. Everyone loves my grandma. Do you love my grandma?"

I'm tired of being a liar. I answer him truthfully. "Yes, I love your grandma." I smile at my grandson whose blue eyes are locked on my own before I add, "Let's go ask her to make us a hamburger."

Swoosh...swoosh. Superhero is on his way.

CHILD
By Paula Timpson

Child,
You are
Forever with me
Shining your light
Into my Soul
Muse, you teach me
How to love and
How to live!!!
Child, your creativity is a blessing~
Every day you lead the way to hope
& new dreams, abandon and peace
What would I do without you?
I really don't know,
Now that you are mine
You are God's child, running wild
You place everyone right into the moment
That is so beautiful, like a painting, free and colorful!
Thank you,
Child for being who you are
Like no one else~
Your heart lights up
Lives, touching upon
What is truly valuable
Simply
Being together…

LIGHT OF MY LIFE
By Terri Elders

The Long Beach Police Department assigned my husband to rotating shifts the year our son, Steve, started first grade. So Bob slept mornings and worked evenings. On weekends often he'd pull a day shift. Our schedules rarely jibed.

"I feel like a single parent," I'd initially complained.

"It won't be forever, so try to make the most of it."

"I suppose I should be grateful that you've got a job, even if you won't be around much."

"You'll love having Steve all to yourself," Bob replied, smiling.

So for three years, from September to June, life flowed predictably. Steve and I would rise, dress, grab breakfast, and go. Steve trotted to his school across the street from our apartment complex. I caught a bus to the high school where I taught English.

At dusk we'd perch together at the kitchen counter. Steve plowed through his homework while I corrected papers. Then we'd sizzle up a batch of Jiffy Pop, and watch *Ozzie and Harriet* or *The Patty Duke Show*. Unless it was the rare night with Bob home, we'd be asleep by 10. The steady plodding backbeat of school bells kept us on track.

In summer our days picked up a jazzier syncopated pace, crammed with options and choices. Frequently we'd ride the bus to the NuPike Arcade at Rainbow Pier, where we'd chuckle with the Laughing Lady who towered over the entrance, or get lost in the maze in the Hall of Mirrors. After stuffing ourselves with Pronto Pups and salt-water taffy, we'd hit the Skee-Ball alleys. Often we'd close our day by treating ourselves to a ride on the double Ferris wheel, where, from the top, we could see all of downtown Long Beach.

Or we'd visit one of the Ocean Boulevard movie theaters. The first time we exited *Mary Poppins* we tried to sing, "Supercalifragilisticexpialidocious" and got it just as wrong as Jane and Michael did in the film. Steve giggled until he hiccupped. Another summer we saw *Born Free*, and Steve ducked his head to hide his tears when Elsa, the lioness, wandered off into the jungles of Meru National Park.

Sometimes we'd just stroll to the nearby library branch to check out stacks of books. Steve had his own library card and favored the *Encyclopedia Brown* mysteries. On the bus trips to the NuPike, the movies, or the park he'd devise possible ways for the clever boy detective to foil his nemesis, Bugs Meany.

If he were on the day shift, Bob would swing by our apartment on his lunch hour to transport us to Recreation Park in his patrol car. We'd pack up sandwiches, and grab a blanket and our books. Steve would play in the sprinklers, climb the monkey bars in the playground, and then plop beside me to discuss Encyclopedia Brown.

After work Bob would join us, bringing along the picnic basket, Coleman lantern and stove, and our portable radio. We'd broil hot dogs, listen to Vin Scully call the Dodger game, and stay until the mercury vapor lamps flickered on. We'd pack our equipment back in the car, and then Steve loved to turn the dial that slowly snuffed out the wick on the gas-powered Coleman lamp.

Bob had been right. I'd enjoyed spending time alone with Steve, witnessing first hand his developing interests, skills, and attitudes. So by the summer of '66 I decided to quit teaching and become a caseworker with Los Angeles County. My evenings and weekends wouldn't be consumed by lessons plans and correcting homework. Though I'd forfeit future lazy summers with Steve, I'd have more time for him year-round. It seemed a fair trade.

Steve knew this would be our last entire summer together.

"Let's go to the beach more this year. I'm going to save my Skee-Ball points for something extra-special."

The previous summer he'd exchanged his points for a Battleship board game…the year before, a GI Joe action figure and a bag of marbles.

"So what's extra-special? A baseball mitt? A chemistry set?"

Steve grinned and shook his head. "Not telling…you gotta guess."

In the '60s, Skee-Ball had not yet gone electronic. With its abbreviated alleys and baseball-sized plastic balls, Skee-Ball appealed to kids too small to bowl, and to the moms who accompanied them to the Pike. Moms formed a queue to snag a free alley while the kids scrutinized display cases filled with potential prizes.

After three summers Steve knew how to bowl his nine balls for maximum effect. He'd even bank some balls against the side of the ramp to try to reach the holes with higher designated point values. His scores steadily improved over the summer.

Shortly before the start of the new school year, Steve and I took our final bus ride to Rainbow Pier.

"I've got a lot of points, Mom. Guess what I'm getting."

"Legos? Roller skates?"

Steve shook his head.

"A Daisy Red Ryder Pump Gun? Lincoln Logs?"

Yet another shake and a giggle.

"An electric train? No? I give up. I'm not Encyclopedia Brown!"

Steve chuckled. "You gave up, so you'll just have to wait and see."

To celebrate summer's end we splurged on a pair of root beer floats at Nathan's. We even took a spin on the famed Looff carousel, even though Steve earlier had protested that at eight he was too old for merry-go-rounds. I insisted that if I weren't too old for a ride, neither was he.

We finally proceeded to the arcade.

"You wait here, Mom."

I watched Steve sprint towards the prize stand, wondering what he'd select. A few minutes later he came back, carrying a bag nearly as big as himself.

"I'll show you what I picked out on our ride home," he said, grinning up at me.

As the bus turned from Ocean Boulevard onto Atlantic Avenue, Steve reached into his bag.

First, he dragged out a Slinky. I knew that popular inexpensive toy would barely take a bite out of his accumulated points. Then he dug in again. "And an Etch-a-Sketch."

I nodded, but I privately wondered if he might have been cheated. I knew he had far more points than those two things could cost.

He glanced at me. "And something else," he whispered. He fumbled around inside the bag, and then pulled out a gaudily painted seashell-encrusted lava lamp.

"I got this for you, Mom," he said. "We've had so much fun at the Pike. The shells will remind you of the beach. And it's turquoise, like the ocean."

That fall I started work as a caseworker, so never again had entire summers free. My husband eventually returned to working normal day shifts. Steve reached the age where he preferred spending weekends playing *Stratego* and *Risk* with the boys next door to taking bus trips with his mom.

Decades later lava lamps became prime examples of '60s kitsch. Mine, though, remained a treasure, an extra-special gift from my extra-special son, until it somehow disappeared in moves from one home to another.

But that incandescent summer of '66 shines on. I'll never forget the warm August sun at the old Long Beach NuPike, and those carefree splashy days with my son…who forever has remained the light of my life.

A CHILD'S IMAGINATION
By Lynn C. Johnston

A child's imagination
Is something special to behold
Inanimate objects come to life
Creating new stories to be told

"Ahoy there, matey," he called out to me
From a cardboard box
"I found some buried treasure, Mom"
His hands full of twigs and rocks

He sings his favorite songs to me
Cause he's a rock star in his mind
And as a mighty Power Ranger
He fights those who live a life of crime

A hockey pro and baseball star
Are what he'd like to be
He leaps and yells pretending
He's Tarzan swinging from a tree

He's a soldier and an astronaut
A Pokémon master in his dreams
A gymnast on the monkey bars
Winning a gold medal for his team

His imagination beckons me
To all that life could be
If I keep on dreaming
Despite whatever I may see

MOTHER-DAUGHTER LOVE
By Elayne Clift

Perhaps it's too much,
this love I bear you.
Intrusive, smothering,
Enough-already love.
(But would you call me
then, from 3,000 miles away
to ask about left-over turkey,
or how long to cook the pasta?)

Shall I tell you where it comes from,
this overwhelming love I've only just
realized was my mother's love for me,
-- and mine for her --
suppressed and garbled
and transmitted via
airwaves crackling with static
emotion and sparks of pain?

This, my child, is mother love,
and daughter love,
hugged into one nurturing,
convoluted embrace.
For loving you,
I enfold myself in my mother's arms
and am loved as I wished to be,
as I love you. As I love her.
And I am at once, hungry and fulfilled,
Mother, Daughter, Love.

WHERE IS MY OFF BUTTON?
By Carolyne Van Der Meer

It's what he asks me in the half-light
laughing with giddy delight at his own
cleverness. The glare from the street casts a
bar across his face, I see the devilish grin

fragmented, see one eye dancing with
mischief. *Find it, mommy!* he challenges me,
Can you find it, please? My fingers slip across
his small body, hesitating over his belly, stopping

on the knot of his navel. *No, that's my on button!* he
says giggling. My own laughter falls in sync with his
as I resort to tickling. *Stop, stop!* he shrieks, rolling
away from me. *Hold me, mommy, just hold me,* he says

suddenly calming. The twilight air catches me in mid-thought:
I think I will forever remember this moment, dog days of
summer, just hours after cheering incessantly through a
baseball game, the magic of the day climaxing in nightfall.

I'm scared, he says, and I am reminded of the fragility of
childhood, the way joy could give way to terror in an instant:
I hold him tight. *Everything is fine,* I say. *We are both
here, daddy and I; there is nothing to be afraid of,* I assure

him, stroking his hair. *What can I think about?* he asks, willing
a good dream on his journey towards sleep. I rhyme off a list,
watching his eyes widen, and his mouth form *oh yes* as
though he had forgotten the endless possibilities for happiness.

ABOUT A SMILE
By Daawy

Eight years ago, I went to Mali on a humanitarian trip organized by my school, 'Institut Le Rosey.' My diary was lost somewhere in my old classroom to gather dust, and the pictures I took from my disposable camera were never returned to me. But what I retained, even with these unfortunate circumstances, is far greater than any recorded writing or an album filled with snapshots. The experience completely took me by surprise and changed my whole perspective on life. There is no wonder why, years later, even as a mother of two children, I still persistently urge my family to travel to Mali, although I know the answer will always be 'no.'

I remember how fortunate I felt to have the opportunity to go to Mali and teach their children English in a developing school called 'Le Rosey –Abantara' in Bamako, the bustling capital city of Mali. The vaccination they gave me to prevent yellow fever seemed like a tiny compromise despite my huge fear of needles. My disgust towards insects appeared insignificant. I fell in love with the greater cause, my mission. It was a dream of mine to teach children and who better than thirsty pupils in dire need of education? Little did I know that I was going to be their student, since the children of Mali provided me unintentionally with the greatest lessons possible— the lessons of life.

It was dry, dusty, and very hot during the 'Fasting Season' of Ramadan. I was fasting with them. I never felt the heat and the drought, as my determination quenched my needs; despite the hours teaching English and playing soccer during recess. Their burning desire to grasp all the information we have taught them was very revitalizing. They spoke in French and I had to translate a lot of words from English to French for them to be able to understand; but like a sponge they absorbed it all in no time.

A group of girls in the school gathered around me in a huddle. They touched my hair in fascination! My long silky tresses stood apart from their midnight black masses of curls. Their thick intricate braids, woven with delicate hands and creative taste, were tied with colorful ribbons, often wrapped with a scarf wound around their heads. They were surprised to learn my real name and I was astounded that my name is more popular in Africa than in my own country! Their school's promoter also brought his first wife to me— just because she and I share the same name! Their amiable qualities and their social skills made me smile and forget that I was standing in one of the world's poorest countries. I felt ashamed for the countless times I grimaced and flashed my face with crumpled smiles, when I had everything I need to lead a comfortable and content life.

Their classrooms were filled with kids ranging from the age of seven to fifteen. Some of the students were lucky to be educated at an early age and others were not that fortunate. The walls were bare and dusty. Book shelves positioned at the back of the classroom were filled with charitable books donated by our school. The floors were packed with wooden tables and chairs. Every little space available was precious. Every little space available saved an illiterate child. It was daunting to realize that these poor children in front of me, with all their modest and humble belongings, were considered 'privileged!' At that moment, being a student myself, I felt that with all the resources available to us in our own school, we should not be satisfied by merely passing. We owed it to ourselves and our parents to pass our classes with flying colors!

Although the very poor wore tattered African tie-dyed and batik fabrics— if they were wearing any— their eyes were filled with glimmering hope and their faces lit up with honest smiles. They smiled with lightness and ease, since they owned the cherished gift of satisfaction; a wealth so great that many of us lack, no matter what background we come from and how much money we have. At that moment, it did not matter to me that the only greenery I noticed was the grass we walked on before I entered their small but impressive ethnographic National Museum, or that the green buses, called *"bâchées vans,"* we rode had ropes for doors; or even that our decent hotel, with all its air-conditioned spacious rooms and marbled floors, lacked ketchup!

Every morning for a week, I would go to their school and teach the children a new lesson in grammar, some vocabularies, and would instruct them to write short sentences in their notebooks. Then, I and my fellow peers would chant the songs we scribbled on the chalkboard. Our students would sing along with us with their soft sweet voices. The dim classroom would suddenly feel vibrant and colorful, as though we formed a choir— performing angelic songs—touching our hearts before our ears.

I blush every time I remember the day I instructed my own English professor not to write all the letters in capitals on the blackboard, because I was trying to teach my Malian friends that only the first letter in a sentence and the proper nouns start with capital letters. He kindly agreed and erased all that he had just written. I was flattered. For the first time, I felt like a real teacher, and that my students and professor took me seriously.

The days passed quickly until it was time to bid my students farewell. Tears were streaming down their once cheerful faces, while their smiles, now drenched with tears, remained intact like a rainbow, strong and powerful amidst showers of rain. The girls started to remove their own African trade beads and accessories, which they bought from the artisans in The Market. They handed them to me as a thank you gift before my departure, along with tiny scraps of paper marked with their home addresses. I did not want to take their jewels! Meeting them was more than enough! However, it would have been rude to return their thoughtful presents, so I accepted them with a shaky voice and smiling tears.

As I reminisce the years that passed like sand cascading from an hourglass, the memory of attending a mask event at night suddenly came alive before my very eyes. I could not focus on the huge artistic costumes and carved wooden elaborate masks the performers skillfully wore. My whole attention shifted to a little boy called Ibrahim, who was not much older than my own son now. He was standing in front me and I, without thought, embraced and showered him with kisses. The next day, little Ibrahim came to search for me. He did not know that I would rather have the Earth devour me, than spend any time dancing publicly, but I gathered all my strength and courage and twirled with him along with other friends and children. We danced to their traditional music and the sounds of their *"Tam-tams"* or drums, reed flutes, and stringed gourd instruments. I did not want the boy to feel left out. For the first time, I did not care how silly I might have appeared or how poorly I performed my dance steps; I actually enjoyed myself!

Not to forget the time I went strolling passed a pink sandstone village shaped into rock faces, when a little bewildered child spotted the flash of my camera. Within minutes, he had called all the children from their low, mud-walled houses and they climbed a tree! They stared at my camera and pointed at it, as I took more pictures. Their smiling faces beamed luminously up at me in fascination. A simple flash for these children was entertainment. Their excitement and enthusiasm was contagious as it streamed through my veins— providing me with genuine comfort and peace of mind, I never felt elsewhere. The photographic memory of that special day portrayed itself in my mind, whenever I see beautiful trees decorated with the freshest finest fruits; I smile, as if to say: "Nothing can beat that wonderful tree of children!"

A sincere mom pulls out a brown leather handmade folder she bought eight years ago from Mali that holds most of her profound memories within. The latch comes off and curious, chubby hands fiddle

the remains of a scarred past. I inhale the scent of oiled leather and dust
and smile at my own son— a smile that hides a million tears underneath.
"Baby," I say, "someday you will come to appreciate all the little things
in life—a sweet smile, a new word, a game of soccer, and a flash from a
disposable camera. Someday you will learn that a kind smile is also
charity and value the power of your little smile!"

GRANDPA WALKS WITH LUNA AT FOUR
By Jim Gustafson

On the forest path
Where we walk
You are perched
On my aging shoulders
We giggle at the birds'
Silly songs
Your hands hold tight
To my thin gray hair

I cannot help
But think ahead
To your prom
So many years
Yet to pass before
You will dress
As a fair maiden
To be taken
Away by a knight
In his father's car

And I, if there is grace,
Will be here
To watch you go
To worry, until I see you again
And you tell me
Almost everything
There is to tell
About the night

BIG GIRL KINDERGARTEN MOMMY
By Debbie Izzi

It was a warm, green Monday morning and the first day of the new school year at Sacred Heart Elementary. First and second graders romped through the just cut grass. Sixth graders struggled to hang the flag. The whistles of proud fifth grade crosswalk patrols shrilled. And the heady scent of hot lunch – pizza – wafted through the air.

My twin boys, Jack and Julian, were starting kindergarten. They huddled together, in their white shirts and pressed pants, looking small. I stood nervously with the other kindergarten moms hoping I had packed enough snacks, worrying about bathroom accidents, and fretting over driving home by myself…without the twins.

My oldest son, Peter, was in third grade so I had experienced a child starting kindergarten before. But Peter, solid and strong as an oak, never really seemed to need me, even as an infant. Jack and Julian were different. Maybe it was because they weighed just two pounds when they were born and spent the first weeks of life in intensive care. Perhaps it was their asthma or the troubles they had learning to talk. Or it could have been that I miscarried a set of twins, right before I became pregnant with Jack and Julian. Whatever the reason, kindergarten was going to be hard on me.

I was about to walk over to Jack and Julian, to press my lips against their soft hair one more time, when a little girl wedged herself between them. Her hair ribbon, pink and blue like the foil around Hershey's kisses, fluttered in the light breeze. Little red heart earrings dangled from her ears.

"I'm Bella. Bella means beautiful," she said and then she prattled on about ladybugs and rainbows. My boys blinked their big brown eyes at her as if she were a creature from outer space.

Jack had no time for ladybugs, rainbows or anything girly and he soon drifted away. Julian, however, was captivated. He smiled, cautiously and mostly at me, but then, more broadly at Bella. He smoothed his hair down and re-tucked his shirt into his pants. By the time the second bell rang, Bella was expertly straightening his collar and showing him how to clasp his hands just so.

That afternoon when I arrived at school to pick up the boys, Julian joyously ran to me, threw his arms around my legs and announced, "I HAVE A GIRLFRIEND!"

Big brother Peter gagged. "Embarrassing! I can NEVER go to school again. Julian was kissing, holding hands, and just being embarrassing with a GIRL!"

Jack whacked Peter with his lunchbox. "She's not a girl! She's Bella. And she's Julian's girlfriend!"

All the way home we discussed Bella: Bella's favorite color was pink, Bella could count to 27, Julian loves Bella, Julian was going to marry Bella, Bella was going to marry Julian, Jack could live with them, and so on. I eyed the twins in the rear view mirror and had to smile at their flushed faces, tomato sauce stained shirts and already torn pants. Maybe this was going to be okay, I thought.

The excitement over Bella almost eclipsed the news that Jack, always the troublemaker in preschool, had continued his reign of terror in kindergarten by kicking someone on the playground. Julian, who had appointed himself Jack's attorney at about age three, assured me it was an accident. He reported that by some cruel trick of gravity, Jack's foot slipped right off the ground, up, up, up into the other boy's belly. It was certainly not Jack's fault in any way, despite what the teacher's note in Jack's backpack said.

"The boy was standing too close to me Mommy!" Jack shouted, "I couldn't breathe!   I was about to die!"

"I don't want Jack to die," Julian said.

We had pulled into the garage by then and Peter leapt from the car snorting loudly. "You both are soooo embarrassing; I'm the one who's going to DIE!"

We returned to school the next morning. Peter raced ahead to join the cluster of third grade boys. The twins followed. A few minutes later, Bella sashayed across the parking lot. Her shiny patent leather Mary Janes slapped against the sidewalk.

"Hi Bella!"   Julian chirped, floating toward her, arms outstretched, face lit up like Christmas morning.

"Oh, no, here it comes!" Peter groaned, rolling his eyes. "More embarrassing kindergarten lovey-dovey stuff."

And that is when Bella laid eyes on Peter. Her lips dropped into a perfect O. Her eyes glowed. Her lashes fluttered. She flew to Peter and threw her arms around him, locking her little fingers around his back.

Peter, horrified, stared up at the hot air balloons drifting overhead, pretending that there was not a kindergarten girl clinging to him like he was a life preserver. Bella rubbed her head on his tummy and smiled blissfully. The other third grade boys, initially stunned into silence, began to snicker. This was too much for Peter. Looking like he was about to lose his pancake breakfast, he struggled to pry Bella's round arms from his body.

"Mommy?" A soft voice said. Julian stared up at me, stricken. "Peter took my girlfriend!" He tugged on my hand and I felt the pull on my heart.

Jack and Julian believed that God lived in Sacred Heart Church, although they admitted they had never actually seen him there. That day, he must have been looking out the window, because just then the first bell rang. Bella's older sister dragged her from Peter and shoved her toward the kindergarten line.

Bella immediately sought out Julian. She flicked her long hair and the air was filled with the sweet scent of strawberry shampoo. Julian pulled his hand from mine and offered it to her. She didn't notice his outstretched fingers.

"I'm sorry, Julian," she said in Marilyn Monroe breathlessness. "I can't be your girlfriend anymore. I'm going to marry your brother Peter. He's in third grade you know!" She whirled around and skipped away.

Jack glared. "Girls are yucky."

Julian's hand fell to his side. His shoulders slumped. I took his trembling body into my arms and laid my cheek on his hair, still damp from the morning bath. He buried his face in my neck and I felt his warm breath on my skin. He smelled like toothpaste and innocence.

The second bell rang, and children clumped past us into class. Julian shook against me as if his whole little self were breaking. I knew he was fighting not to cry, as he was a big boy kindergartener. I too, was trying not to cry, as I was a big girl kindergarten mommy.

"Mommy, you're my girlfriend – you'll always be my girlfriend – right?" he asked.

I wanted to scoop him and Jack up, like I used to when they were babies – a twin in each arm - race back to the car and drive away. Far away from girlfriends, morning bells and broken hearts.

But I didn't do that. I couldn't.

I used to think that the hardest part of being a mom was taking care of babies. But I had begun to see that all that was easy compared to just letting my children go. There was so much I couldn't protect them from.

"I'll always be yours, Julian." I whispered.

Jack nudged Julian, "Come on Julian," he said. "Who needs stupid girls?"

He belched loudly. Julian turned to him and burped back. Jack threw his arm around Julian's shoulders and they walked away. Their laughter rang out across the schoolyard – young and strong and in a way, invincible.

      I knew then that while I couldn't always protect Jack and Julian, they would be okay. They could take care of each other. And that meant I would be okay too.

67

KEVIN DANCING
By Karen Ethelsdattar

Little grandson,
you were dancing
almost before you could walk,
your head bobbing,
your hands clapping,
your small sturdy body swaying
to melodies,
beating out rhythms.
Now your mother tells me that
your dog Gus was lapping up
his water
& you picked up the rhythm
& began to bop to it.

Surely you're *my* grandchild
dancing to your dog lapping water,
splashing in your bath,
turned on to the way
the whole world is singing.

I WILL LONG FOR THIS ONE DAY
By Carolyne Van Der Meer

Will I remember this always? I will long for it
one day, the smell of must in your hair
from sweat and sleep, the molding of your
small scrawny body into mine as we sit on a fading
porch chair early, sun barely awake. You come to
say good morning, mumble I love you, grains of sleep
in your eyes, fold backward, into me, then scurry to
watch cartoons.

ANGEL DREAMS
By Louise Webster

A full moon is out
My baby asleep
Wispy blonde hair
Dreaming deep

Cupid lips purse gently
A tiny angel kiss
Free from every worldly care
She soothes the universe

WAITING
By Sharon Medoff Picard

Waiting at the airport, as a college son departs
I watch the plane, observing…
Convinced in that love-filled place within me that is beyond reason
That if I watch the silver plane lumber to the runway and rise to the sky
Under my watchful eye,
> All will be well.

I am reminded of other times and other places
When my mother-sense defies all other sense
And keeps me,
Watching, scanning, peering,
As years of school buses, cars, trains and planes roll by carrying a
precious child,
Somehow, secure and safe
> As long as we are bound by the magic of my vigil.

AN ANGEL'S LESSON
By Suzanne Manning

My niece, who is also my godchild, is now 16 years old. My sister-in-law never had any type of amniocentesis testing before she was born, so none of us had any idea that she would be born with special needs. My mother and I went to visit my niece in the hospital just after she had been born; no one had time to tell us that she had been born with Down's Syndrome until we arrived at their hospital room. We weren't able to hold her for the first time because the nurses had taken her for testing. The doctors were concerned about heart problems and other problems that she could have been born with, but ultimately wasn't.

We left my sister-in-law's hospital room without being able to see my niece and I remember being in shock. I had no experience at that time with a child who had special needs, or, any type of challenge for that matter. During the ride home through Boston, the car was silent, not a word was spoken between my mother and I. I remember staring out at the lights amongst the city, worrying for my new niece. What challenges would she face in life, would people pick on her because she was different? I started to cry and the silence in the car had been broken. My mother, a retired Newborn Nursery Nurse herself, finally spoke up when she heard me inhaling between the tears. "You're not crying for her, you're crying for yourself you know, she's going to be fine."

My niece was blessed with the best mother a child born with special needs could have, so pro-active, immediately getting early intervention in place for her new baby, physical therapy, everything the baby needed to succeed in life. We were all truly blessed to have this beautiful, loving, amazing child in our life. Like an angel sent to us from heaven above.

Fourteen years later, my niece, a vibrant typical boy-crazy, music-loving teenager, was loving high school, her friends and activities that were still in place for her, until one day we received an incredibly devastating blow. My niece was diagnosed with leukemia.

A complete double whammy is what my first reaction was. This poor kid had enough challenges in life, but to be diagnosed with a cancerous disease as well. I was enraged and confused. Who else could I take it out on but God? Besides, I figured this was all his doing anyway.

I visited my niece in the hospital as much as possible while she was hospitalized for two months due to critical complications caused by the leukemia and chemotherapy. Visiting within the pediatric cancer unit of the hospital and the pediatric intensive care unit, at times took its toll on me. It was if I had entered a war zone.

I myself did some serious soul searching during this whole ordeal and did not want to give up on my beliefs, faith, and hope, but I was still so angry inside and still just as confused as to how this could happen not just to my niece, but any child. Watching her struggle shattered my faith and I stopped attending church altogether.

But my niece's faith had not been shaken, not once, throughout this whole ordeal. I gave her a necklace that my uncle had a woman make for him. It was a bead made out of a single rose petal. The bead was the angel's body and attached where silver wings. When I presented my niece with the necklace, she told me it reminded her of Jesus, and that Jesus was not her friend, he was her savior. When she was baptized as an infant, I took a spiritual vow as her Godmother to teach her about God, and to keep God in her life. But now the tables were turned and she was teaching me. She had opened my eyes, my faith, and belief yet again.

I had realized then that God had been there all along and he was all around us. I saw him in the faces of my niece's doctors who had saved her life not once, but twice. I saw him in the faces of the nurses that would try to make the children laugh while they underwent their treatments; the nurses that were always so gentle and kind. I saw him in the faces of the volunteers that would come to do arts and crafts with the kids or visit with the therapy dogs. I saw him in the face of my niece's pastor and his family who would come to her hospital room to pray with her.

But most of all I saw him in the eyes of my sister-in-law, her mother, who fought with everything she had with a loving heart to stay right by her side, caring for her every need. I saw him in the eyes of my brother who loves his angel; she is truly Daddy's angel. I saw him in the eyes of her brother and sister who have stood by their sister's side all the way.

Isn't it true that we are supposed to try and be more like God in our everyday lives, kind, gentle, forgiving, non judgmental? Well, these people that I speak of, who have been in the front lines and have fought this disease are the closest to him that I have seen by far. I feel so foolish now that I had ever questioned my faith, but I think some of us do at times. Now, I see God so much more than I ever did before. There are still people who care, are compassionate, and love wholeheartedly.

My niece is now in remission, still boy crazy, loves music and singing, and still attends school and all of her activities. I guess my mother was right, as she usually is, I was crying for myself, not for my niece, she was going to be fine. Please, keep the faith.

GOOD VERSUS EVIL
By Susan Mahan
(Super Nana)

At the age of four,
my grandson Ethan has it all figured out.

He's in a Super Hero phase,
dressing up as Batman and zooming around the house,
watching his Superfriends videos,
convincing me to wear a Superman costume
to his birthday party.

Ethan knows without question
which guys are good and which are bad.
He says that he and I are good guys.

I wish that life could always be that clear.

COLLEGE MAN
By Ann Reisfeld Boutté

When he leaves home
I'll have time
to read my stack of books,
stitch my needlepoint pillow,
put photos in an album,
reorganize the pantry,
munch on salted popcorn
at a weekday matinee.

But what I'd rather do is
see him every morning,
pick up his dirty socks,
endure his techno music,
be his short-order cook,
listen to his stories
and catch traces in his smile
of yesterday

when we spent hours
at the playground,
toured the streets on bikes,
picked wildflowers for our table,
built castles in the sandbox.
He was sunshine I could cuddle
and I was his girl.

THE HEALER
By Liz Dolan

Four-year-old David who has Downs
snuggles into three-year-old

Tommy's chest like a Maine coon cat.
Then he pets Tommy's head

flubs his lips on his pale cheek
and laughs at the noise it makes

with so much heart, he warms ours.
Even though he knows Tommy

cannot move nor speak, unlike us
he does not give up hope for him

maybe recalling when he himself
sipped air raggedly through a treach

and could not pedal his trike
but how last night in falling twilight

he did.

DREAM FOR JOEL
(Circle of Life)
By Tom Leskiw

A number of loose ends required our attention before we could depart our winter home in Arizona to return to Northern California. They included writing, woodworking, landscaping projects, phoning various utilities to suspend or transfer service, and finally, loading and hitching the canoe trailer to our vehicle.

In the crush, I'd managed to backburner my grief over the failing health of our dog, Gypsy. Despite being 13 years old, she'd been the picture of health a mere four months before, when we'd traveled south. Then, one night, we found her blind and drooling. She seemed to have lost her sense of smell and some of her coordination. It had been nearly 40 years since I'd owned a dog. The loss of a trusted, long-time companion cuts deep, as painful then as it is now.

We'd elected to make a minor detour on our route through southern California. Sue's Aunt Ann was nearly 91 years old. Looking in on someone that you've known for that long is always the right thing to do. Ann's dog Pixie didn't like other dogs, so it would take a bit of work keeping Gypsy and her separated.

The next morning, we sat in the backyard with Ann and her son Alan, talking and playing catch-up. I had trouble concentrating on the conversation, as waves of grief periodically washed over me. Even in my present state, though, I had to acknowledge signs of spring, of a world awakening from its winter slumber. Soaring by in a northwest direction was a kettle of migrating Turkey Vultures, riding the late-morning thermals. Scores of bees worked the blossoms of a *Myoporum* tree. A purple bejeweled male Costa's Hummingbird made frequent visits to the feeder. Painted lady butterflies sped past us flying north, pausing here and there to sip nectar from trees and shrubs. These glimpses into the Circle of Life comforted me, for their movements continued unabated, each of these creatures sensing that it was their time.

The phone rang. It was a neighbor informing us that they could hear Gypsy howling from the front courtyard. Gypsy was silent when I approached her. Head trembling, her clouded eyes were staring into nothingness, which communicated life's precious and transitory nature. I sat down next to her, my eyes filling with tears as I submitted to the waves. Some time later, I opened my eyes to see a young boy and girl on their bikes, just outside the gate.

"My name's Joel," said the boy. "We heard your dog howling, so my parents phoned to tell you..." The boy came closer to the gate and reached out, trying to pet Gypsy.

"I wouldn't do that," I warned. "Gypsy's blind and it will startle her."

He withdrew his hand and paused. "Why is your dog blind?" he asked. At that moment, my thoughts were so consumed by darkness and the fragility of life, all I could think of to say was, "Because everything gets old and sick and then it dies." But, of course, I didn't—I couldn't—say that. His question was a sincere one and, on a gorgeous spring day that held so much promise, who was I to upset him?

"We're not sure," I responded. "One day she was fine. It happened all at once."

He looked at me with earnest eyes and then at Gypsy. The expression on his face stopped short of challenging what I'd said, but I could tell he didn't totally believe me, either. As if on cue, Gypsy stumbled off the sidewalk into landscaping—knocking over a long metal handle that controlled the sprinkler valve. It landed with a clatter onto the sidewalk and I could tell that Joel was now convinced of her condition.

I couldn't help but be reminded of the lyrics to a David Crosby song, "Dream for Him." The song was prompted by a car ride Crosby took with his young son. While driving, he reflects on what he'll tell his son, should they come across a car wreck where the occupants have died. What's the correct way to introduce the young and innocent to a dark subject like death?

Joel turned to his sister. Whether to break the awkward silence or to commiserate with me, he offered, "Yeah, we know a one-eyed dog." While he and his sister rode circles in Ann's driveway, Joel and I chatted. I kept things light—not a word about the mortality of people and dogs. "We know this yard," he shared with me, a declaration of his haunts, a disclosure that Ann's yard and driveway lay within the territory explored by his sister and him on their bikes.

As Joel and I made small talk in the warm spring sunshine, I studied his face and thought about how he and his sister had their whole lives ahead of them. Hopefully, their existence had yet to be tainted by life's unpleasantries. Their future was one of infinite possibility. And I thought about how—even though we'd just met—I had a dream for him: the same, or similar, one I have for every child I encounter:

May you be cared for and mentored by people who love you dearly. My wish for you is to always have the freedom to investigate life's mysteries, to expand your present horizons. May you reap the best that life has to offer and reach your full potential. I hope that your days include lazy afternoons, lying in tall, overarching grass with your dog at your side. I wish for you to be awestruck that such an amazing dog is your companion, one who wants nothing more from you than to love and be loved in return. And, in an odd way—bear with me, now—I also wish you grief. Because, as painful as it is, grief is a kind of Certificate of Authenticity, proof that you've lived and loved, not merely observed life from the sidelines.

The next day, we had a couple of hours to visit with Alan and Ann before we'd have to hit the road. We pulled several lawn chairs into a circle on the front lawn next to a densely-branched cedar tree and talked. Sue pointed out a pile of feathers beneath the tree. Looking over the pile, I noted that it contained an array of feathers—larger ones from tail and wing, in addition to a puffy cluster of small, buoyant, downy feathers. I examined a tri-colored tail feather: dark gray at the base, narrow black band near the middle, and a wider, pale-gray band at the tip. The description of the tail feather matched that of the numerous Eurasian-collared Doves in the neighborhood. I surmised that a predator—probably a Cooper's Hawk—had killed, plucked, and then eaten the dove while perched in the cedar tree.

Sue, Ann, and Alan posed for several photos. Later, Alan left for his volunteer shift and Sue and Ann went inside to make lunch, while I kept an eye on Gypsy. Suddenly, I heard the tell-tale low-frequency hum of an Anna's Hummingbird coming from the middle of the cedar tree. It took me awhile to locate the bird, but when I did, I watched as it hover-descended slowly toward the ground. When it was only an inch or two from the ground, it reached out and snatched in its bill a downy feather.

Then, it burst from the protective embrace of the cedar limbs and buzzed down the street, veering sharply to avoid a parked camper. I strained to keep the tiny bird in view as it disappeared into a row of pines. *Lining its nest with downy feathers... I've only seen hummingbirds carrying nest materials on two other occasions... Circle of Life. How cool is that?*

This stark reminder that new life can spring from death served as a tonic. And, thanks to my conversation with Joel, I vowed to try to adopt a child's perspective—that the future holds limitless possibilities and that my best days were ahead of me.

AUTUMN
By Carol L. Gloor

Even though people don't let a little girl
walk to school alone anymore,
alone in her Catholic plaid skirt
and stuffed backpack,

here she is — in white sleeves too short
for this chill October morning,
hurrying herself to St. Gertrude's,
four blocks away,

her hair swinging
under flaming maples.
She's nine, maybe ten. I'm fifty-four,
a block behind, but gaining.

She's been taught well, stops
at every street and alley, looking both ways.
Maybe the car pool failed, the schedule missed,
dad overslept.

But even under these sunny trees
I still know the lesson of the years.
I follow her at the right distance,
keeping watch.

MY SON GAVE ME A HUG TODAY
By Susan Siegel

My son gave me a hug today.
Signs of affection,
He usually does not display.
.

Gave me such joy,
It was such a surprise!
When I asked him why,
"I could see it in your eyes."

A special thing between us,
Our mother-son bond.
Difficult times we've had,
I wish I had a magic wand.

To be the perfect mother,
Know the things to do.

Sometimes I want a "redo,"
To start it all again.
But now he stands before me,
He is now almost a man.

Once a baby in my arms,
Now he stands above me.
My son gave me a hug today,
He helped me find my way.

THE PINK NICKEL CLUB
By Elaine Dugas Shea

Christmas is about giving...everyone knows that. But one year we got a better idea of what this holiday was really about. After celebrating Thanksgiving, our children decided to plan on their own for Christmas. Deva and her little brother Johnny dragged out all their special equipment for the first official meeting of the Pink Nickel Club. They used fat markers to schedule meeting dates on the *Snoopy* December calendar. Meetings were held either under the basement stairs where they chalked in secret code on concrete walls *or* in Deva's room, where, in excited whispers, they created Christmas. I *was* curious, but soon learned the Pink Nickel Club was off-limits to parents!

In the beginning, Deva found a plastic treasure chest with a tiny gold lock and key. One of the club's cardinal rules was to bring a nickel to meetings. As Christmas magic might have it, the first nickel had an odd pinkish tint. She counted club dues often to determine what they needed for holiday activities and noted it in the club diary. Deva reminded Johnny to hurry home after school. "You'd better not spill the beans either about what we're doing at Pink Nickel," she added, in a bossy, big-sister way.

Every evening we heard sweet voices rehearsing carols and holiday songs - Deva playing flute, Johnny ringing bells –working to stay on key. Sometimes, he'd frown and grow frustrated. "Deva, I can't do it like you," he'd blurt out. So they practiced harder, memorized verses and repeated *Good King Wenceslaus* reaching near perfection. Both kids decorated Christmas Carol songbooks with crayon designs during arts & crafts time. I managed to sneak hot cocoa and graham crackers on a tray outside the club door. Didn't really eavesdrop, but heard sounds and muted conversations, the swish of paper being cut and wrapped - I guessed this was Pink Nickel Club business. Of course, it *was* a secret. That was the best part.

When we got home from church on a snowy Montana Christmas Eve, Deva and Johnny grinned as they handed us a framed invitation to the Christmas "Pink Nickel" show. In candle glow and hushed silence, we witnessed duets with precise hand motions, flute, bells – - clear, happy voices. Time slowed everything and everyone.   I didn't let them see my tears, but I'm sure Bill's eyes were watery too watching their priceless gift.   We hugged and smiled in amazement.

For many holidays following, the children continued Pink Nickel Club activities. From saved nickels came fruit, cookies, holiday candy and forever memories. Club projects glittered with bright wrapping paper, yarn and ribbon, tissue and sticky stars.   Their surprise performance was the Christmas message of love – a gift from pure hearts that money could not purchase – unless, of course, you belonged to the Pink Nickel Club. Their drawings and chalk words remain etched on our basement walls; proof to this day the Pink Nickel Club lives.

ONCE UPON A BIRTH
For Paxon
By Janet Tamez

Once upon a birth,
The moon round and full, knew it was time
so she urged the sea out of the womb

The Earth trembled
Head, shoulders, knees, and toes...
until she bore a son

His proud chest expanded
His arms beamed like rays

Eyes, ears, mouth, and nose

The wind wailed into his lungs
The fire kept him warm
The skies thundered with his cries, creating a rainbow for his soul

The universe danced around him
Head, shoulders, knees, and toes

Father was pleased and Mother was grateful
Eyes, ears, mouth, and nose

MEMORY
By Raven Sisco

Their feet prance on plush moss
As eyes shimmer in moonlight.
Night yawns above the horizon.
My children dance under stars

Until they carve initials in bark
As small leaves flutter on oaks.
Beaming below shining heaven,
I will remember this moment.

FASHION STATEMENT
For Owen Kirchner — age 4
By Jason Miller

This is when I learned
I loved you —
you changed your clothes,
then asked:
Do these socks rhyme?

I'd never met a child
who dressed so
poetically correct.

SAVING THE TOOTH FAIRY
By Beckie A. Miller

In our home the tooth fairy who had previously resigned duties after our first two children were grown, came out of retirement as we began our parenting years over again. Our new daughter, Kimberlie, who stripped the title of youngest from her nineteen-year-old sister, Christie, to those who don't know any better might be thought of as an 'oops' child. We adopted her, so a lack of not being planned is simply not involved, only careful choices of the heart.

As compared with how much her older brother and sister received for their lost teeth, twenty-five cents, she now receives a crisp one dollar bill. It is probably not quite keeping up with the rate of inflation, but she is happy. The only time she did complain was when the 'tooth fairy,' who on this particular round of raising our kids, happens to be my husband, Don, forgot to claim the tooth and leave the money tucked under her pillow before he turned in for the night. Since I head to bed shortly after my daughter, energy level not being what it once was, I have relinquished the responsibility of my tooth fairy duties this time around.

The next morning I was reading the newspaper and sipping my own recipe of chocolate peppermint coffee, peacefully enjoying the silent time before anyone else in the house awakened, when my quiet reverie was instantly disrupted as I heard a loud scream and saw Kimberlie running towards me.

"Mommy, she shrieked. The tooth fairy forgot my tooth!" She was choking back tears of dismay.

This caused me to immediately assess the situation and jump into mommy-fix-this-one mode. Not to brag, but in true super-mom-fashion and without skipping a beat I might add, I calmly covered with a scenario that the tooth fairy probably saw she was sleeping so soundly, arms wrapped tightly around her pillow that the tooth fairy did not have the heart to awaken her.

I then proceeded to put in place part two of my child's emotional trauma rescue and proverbial saving of my dear husband's 'butt.' I wrote a note (disguising my hand writing just in case my daughter got suspicious) from the tooth fairy to her explaining just the scenario I had given her.   I also added the part of the tooth fairy telling Kimberlie in the note, which by the way had her dollar enclosed, that because the fairy could not reach her tooth without waking her that she could keep the tooth as a special memento for herself.   I then carefully placed the note on the floor by her bed, hoping when she made the bed, she would find it and believe she had knocked it off in her sleep.

That was exactly what happened, thanks to my intervention and careful, though spur of the moment planning.   Kimberlie was absolutely thrilled to be able to keep her tooth.   She even took it to school, along with the infamous note to share with her first-grade classmates and her teacher.

Of course, when my husband got up later that morning, I could not wait to admonish him for forgetting his tooth fairy duties and then, when the look of dismay on his flushed face mirrored our daughter's earlier one of being forgotten, let him off the hook.   I explained I had covered quite nicely for him.   Upon hearing her daddy was up, Kimberlie ran in and could not wait to share her special keepsake with him.

"Daddy!   Look what the tooth fairy left me, a dollar, and my tooth to keep," she exclaimed with pride.

Oh, dearest little one, if only you knew what we moms have to go through sometimes to save our children hurt, I thought to myself, hating that I could not take credit for her joy.   That's okay for now, though.   Someday, I will share this story with her when she is long past her time of childhood innocence and emotional ties to the tooth fairy.   It will bring us much laughter in years to come when recalled.

Parenting always keeps you on your toes.   It is just that my husband's and my toes are not as spry as they used to be and that makes for some challenges and near disasters more often than our younger counterparts might experience, however, it balances out with our mature wisdom!

I tease my husband though, since I am seven years younger than he is, I will continue to cover for him whenever necessary.   He also knows, to his ultimate chagrin, that I will never let him live this episode down -- I consider it my wifely duty.   After all, I have my daughter's emotional well-being to consider as well as saving the reputation of the tooth fairy for generations of kids to come!

HALLOWEEN, 2005
To Samantha, Sixteen
By Pamela L Laskin

You are the princess
who pranced on a white horse,
happy to dance
without a king.
You are the queen
who rules
without a crown,
though sometimes
you are a spirit
especially sixteen years ago
when you twisted my tummy into believing
you were real,
when I thought,
you were just a trick
my body was playing-
big belly
baby inside
but then you were born
beautiful.

And each day
is Halloween,
whatever costume
you dream
it's a treat
watching you wear it.

WHAT JOY A DAUGHTER
Sonnet XXVIII
By James Vasquez

What joy a daughter brings a father's heart.
Her utt'rance of a single word inspires,
That he might be the father, whole and part,
She daily needs, looks up to and desires.

What strength her radiant presence fully grants
To shield, sustain and guide her in the way.
What thankfulness a father's woe supplants,
While tedium's impotence her needs allay.

And absent, so much more the pleasure known
At last, when held within the arms she's found,
For then 'tis clear their love has only grown,
'Tween man and daughter, timelessly close bound.

This gift from high above is giv'n to man,
No greater has there been since time began.

THE PROCLAMATION OF A THREE-YEAR-OLD
By Kellye Blankenship

The moment had arrived. The proclamation declared at our supper table was uttered with enlightened confidence. Hannah is her name. She arrived just a short three years ago and has reassured us daily that "God Given" surprises will forever be unsurpassed.

Evenings are routinely filled with homework, chores, dinner and baths. The aroma of fried chicken circulating throughout the house carried me back to a small kitchen where you could find my mother at least three times a day. Sweat beads would form on her brow as she prepared our meals, even in the winter months.
Her love, I would never question.

My thoughts were interrupted by a small voice, "When is it going to be ready?"

The call to supper created immediate response, unlike bath and bedtime. Plates were filled, tea was poured, and each claimed their place around the large oak table. Hannah announced that we should not eat until someone has said the lesson. That lesson, of course, could also be translated as the prayer of thanks. Surely, you knew that. And so with the food blessed and the echo of Amen, our family began to share the events of the day over a wonderful Southern meal, which, by the way, included mashed potatoes, as did every evening meal.

For a moment consider going to the cabinet to pick out a glass for your drink, do you have a favorite? Well, Hannah has many favorites, so on this particular night I had carelessly placed the "un" favorite spoon on Hannah's plate. As she brought this to my attention she proceeded to make her way to the kitchen to replace the unwanted spoon. As she passed my chair she informed me she would be in need of five spoons instead of just one. You see I had recently purchased some very colorful spoons that I thought she might like. She did indeed, so much, that it was next to impossible to choose just one.

"Hannah, you will only need one," I used my deep motherly voice. "I really will need all of them," she followed with more confidence than a child of three years should possess. So I did what was necessary, with a slow calmness and steady voice I repeated, "Only one."

"Alright," was mumbled using four syllables. Her head hung a little lower as it slowly shifted from side to side. She returned to the table with only one spoon in hand.

Fewer words were shared as the evening mealtime advanced. Hannah had been exceptionally quiet and to be rather honest, that was and is a rare occurrence. But then it happened. She sat up straight in her chair, cleared her throat, and announced what had become outright apparent due to earlier events. We listened as she spoke. "If you ask, you get told NO but if you don't ask, you get to do what you want," with those words she returned to eating her mashed potatoes with her one spoon.

I would love to tell you that we took that teachable moment and utilized it to the fullest measure. We didn't. Instead, we laughed, not the chuckle kind, the kind that causes you to cry and choke on your chicken.

She processed the situation, analyzed, studied, and came to a conclusion. At just the young age of three, learning is taking place. Careful, our children are listening, watching and learning. We have a large responsibility to ensure they see and hear only the good and honorable. "How?" The answer is really very simple, be good and honorable examples. They will follow.

A few short days had passed and I found myself in the kitchen with Hannah. She had managed to talk her sister Schelbye, into making her a bowl of cereal. The bowl had been prepared and awaited her arrival at the table. I stood closely by as I watched Hannah gathering her five new spoons. So I nicely reminded her, "You only need one Hannah." As she closed the drawer, five spoons in hand, she looked up at me and ever so sweetly replied, "I'm not asking."

MOTHER'S DEVOTION
By Carol Rhodes

Oatmeal and milk toast to soothe an upset tummy,
comforting kisses on a bumped head's throb,
scraped knees, first haircut, tooth fairy, first bike,
peanut butter sandwiches under a tree in the back yard,
        slaying dragons under the bed.

Sugar cookies, apple juice, walks in the park,
fried chicken, mashed potatoes, chocolate cake,
baths with bubbles and plastic ducks,
bedtime stories, prayers, kisses goodnight,
        slaying dragons under the bed.

Kindergarten, summer camp, swim meets,
sail boats, football games, high school graduation,
college, first car, first job, wedding, first house,
hugs of consolation when the marriage went awry.
        Still slaying dragons under the bed.

LEARNING LOVE
By Cherise Wyneken

"Nighty-night," said Isabel
to her little doll.
She covered it with care
as she laid it
on the bed.
A kiss, a tuck, a lullaby.
Where did she learn to love?

"Nighty-night," said Mama
to little Isabel.
Warm clean sheets and covers
waited – welcoming her curly head.
A kiss, a tuck, a lullaby.
Where did she learn to love?

"My peace I leave with you,"
said our loving Lord.
"Let not your heart be troubled;
don't worry for tomorrow;
trust in me instead."
A kiss, a tuck, a lullaby.
That's where they learned to love.

KING ME
By Bridget McNamara-Fenesy

"King Me!" he shouted, his grin spilling into his eyes.

The old man had come to love these evenings on the porch with Charlie. He had long since given up letting him win – the boy was a natural, just like his Dad. Like father, like son, like son.

"Granddaddy?"

"Hmm?" he replied, absorbed in finding his next move.

"What happens to you when you die?"

He looked up from the board, and saw the smile was no longer there. "That's a big question for a small boy."

"My Sunday school teacher says we go to heaven and sit at the right hand of Jesus."

"What do you think about that?"

"Sounds pretty boring to me." said the boy. "I don't want to *sit* for all eternity. I want to run, play ball, and eat as much blue cotton candy as I want. But what do you think, Granddaddy?"

"Well, Charlie, nobody really knows for sure what happens when you die. But I can tell you what I believe. I think we don't really die at all. What I see when I look at you, Charlie, is not just your blonde hair and freckles, the way you look like your mother when you're thinking too hard, and how tall you are growing. When I look at you, I see how funny you are, how much you love your dog Teaser, and how your eyes twinkle when you smile. Those things don't die. Those things are part of your soul, and your soul lives on after you die."

"How can that be, Granddaddy? Dad told me when Grandma died that her body just got too old and tired to keep going. But now you're saying that Grandma isn't really dead. If that's true, where is she?"

"Grandma's body is gone, Charlie. After we die, we don't need our bodies anymore. It's like when you grow over the summer, and then you get ready to go back to school, your hair is too long and your arms and legs are pushing out of your clothes because they don't fit. You've grown out of them – you don't need them anymore."

"Grandma out-grew her body?"

"In a way, yes. What was really important about Grandma had nothing to do with her body. What's the one thing you remember most about Grandma?"

"Her awesome warm cherry pie with melting ice cream on top!"

"… and what about the time she made you feel better when you fell off your bike? And how she told you that you would get the hang of it…"

"…and I did! finished Charlie.

"That's right Charlie. You did. You did because Grandma made you feel safe and loved and able to do anything. And you still have that part of her. You were loved by Grandma, Charlie, and that is part of her soul. And that part of Grandma will never die."

"But Granddaddy, what part of you is going to live on after you die?"

"What do you think, Charlie?"

"Well, maybe that you taught me to put a worm on a fishing hook. And the way you smell like the campfire and bacon after we go camping together. And our games of checkers at night."

They had been so engrossed in their chat they did not realize it had fallen dark. They were interrupted by Charlie's mom telling him it was time to get ready for bed.

"That sounds about right, Charlie. That's the part of me that will live on after I'm gone. Because that's love. And love never dies."

"Maybe that's what heaven is Granddaddy – maybe it's just all the things you love, all in one place forever."

"That sounds about right too, Charlie. Maybe it is."

IMPRESSIVE IMAGINATIONS
By Cona F. Gregory-Adams

In the Preschooler's room,
the children were becoming unruly.
The teacher drew an imaginary TV
on the wall with his finger.
"Let's watch *Sesame Street*," he said.

Children sat quietly,
gazing at the wall,
followed by animated descriptions
of the characters on the show,
and what they were doing.

A small boy stood up.
"I'm bored," he said.
"I'm changing the channel."

"No, no," voices chorused.
"Don't change it."
"You can't."
"We're watching this!"

A CAPPELLA
By Ann Reisfeld Boutté

My husband whispers,
"Come here, listen."
An urgent note
quickens my step
.

Head-to-head
by a closed door,
we strain to hear
fragments of melody,
snatches of lyric.

Our teenage son
sings in the shower,
his voice unfettered,
joyful, free.

Never mind tone or timbre.
No tenor, no choir, no songbird
ever made sweeter music.

A FIELD SOMEWHERE
By Harry P. Noble

His name was Billy—nothing more.   We were in the second grade; I was seven and he was ten.   He was held over, but I moved on so we were classmates only one year.

Our school was located in East Texas across the Sabine River from western Louisiana.   Miss Penbrook was the teacher.   Grades one through eleven were offered.   Most of the parents were cotton farmers; the year was 1936.

Billy was tall, but thin.   Classmates said he disappeared when he turned sideways.   His eyes never opened fully and seldom had a need to blink.   He was dispassionate but his overall appearance was happy.   He could smile, sometimes for no reason, but was denied the feeling of excitement.   Much slower than his peers, if a threat materialized he walked away.

The family didn't have money to see a doctor so Billy's inability to learn had never been diagnosed.   When forced by concerned friends to talk about it, his family reverted to such terms as "slow" and "he'll grow out of it."

Billy was called 'dummy,' 'dopey,' 'retard' and other epithets. Most of the time, it was just the candidness or ignorance of youth. Words didn't seem to hurt Billy.   I never saw him react to a cruel phrase. If he had a protective shield, it was kindness.   He spoke softly in short phrases without embellishments.

Billy was a late child and a difficult birth, leaving his mother in a wheelchair.   His father, an older man, ran a general store just off campus. Because Billy's mother required so much of his father's time, his store sales no longer cleared a profit.   Too old for manual labor, not enough money to afford help for his invalid wife, and very little time left to look after Billy's needs; Billy's dad was almost shirtless on a road to nowhere. What little he was able to do for his wife and son, was all that stood between him and Taps.

Sensitive and compassionate to Billy's disorder, Miss Penbrook was providing day care for Billy in her second grade.   She allowed him to sit at any vacant desk, let him stand in spelling bees while always giving him the word 'cat' to spell, and periodically left different books on his desk.

Our school didn't have plumbing, just two outdoor toilets: one for the girls and one for the boys. In class when someone had to go that person raised a hand and asked to be excused. To the envy of classmates Billy didn't have to follow this procedure. He just got up, walked out, and remained gone as long as he liked.

One of the perks students could earn for exceptional work was ringing the school bell for the lunch period or when school was out in the afternoon. In Miss Penbrook's unrelenting efforts to keep Billy involved, she sent him to ring the bell. He went to the bell closet, grabbed the rope, and began to ring. After an interval of time, it suddenly dawned on Miss Penbrook the bell was still ringing. She became concerned, and being aware Billy seemed to trust me, she asked that I go tell Billy that was enough. When I reached the bell closet I said, "Billy, that's enough." He stopped, said, "I like you," and followed me out of the bell closet.

Another perk students could earn was 'dusting the erasers.' As the chalkboards were erased, the chalk dust accumulated in the erasers. When full they smeared instead of erasing and had to be taken outside and beaten against a fence post until all the dust was removed. During a short mental lapse Miss Penbrook assigned this task to Billy. He had been gone a while with two loaded erasers when suddenly she realized he hadn't returned. Sending a student to check on him, the entire class broke into laughter when he returned with Billy who was covered from head to toe with white chalk dust. Miss Penbrook hushed the laughter but the student emissary continued to giggle as he explained that Billy had beaten the erasers against himself instead of the post. Billy remained chalk white the rest of the day.

In the 1930's the large Sears and Roebuck catalog had several pages of John Deere tractors. One day during recess I mentioned something about a John Deere. Billy's face brightened as he reached in his overalls pocket, came out with a hand full of pictures and handed them to me. There were six pictures, all John Deere tractors cut from the Sears catalog.

"What are these, Billy?"

"Mine," Billy said, pointing his finger at himself.

"You own six tractors?" I asked.

He nodded, his eyes alive with a sparkle I'd never seen before.

"Do you plow with all six of them?"

He nodded again.

"What are you raisin'?"

"Cotton," he answered.

Surprised, I didn't know what to say. Finally, after several questions he couldn't answer, I heard myself ask, "Do your tractors have names?"

He nodded.

Holding out a picture of the largest tractor, I asked, "What's the name of this tractor?"

He pointed to the picture and said, "That's George Washington."

I caught my breath as I held out the second largest picture. "Name this one."

He pointed at the second largest tractor--"John Adams." Then the third largest-- "Thomas Jefferson." The fourth--"James Madison." Fifth--"James Monroe."   And the smallest tractor--"John Quincy Adams."

I was overwhelmed and asked a ton of questions about the pictures and his tractors. Billy didn't give many answers because most of the questions were out of his reach, but I did learn he carried those pictures all the time and were pictures of his tractors he was using to grow a cotton crop in a field somewhere. I also discovered he had never shown the pictures to anyone. I thought I knew why he named his tractors after United States presidents; Miss Penbrook had recently passed out a list of our presidents and required everyone (except Billy) to recite them in order while standing in front of the class. That prompted me to ask, "Can you name all of our presidents?"

He didn't answer. I had gone where he couldn't go.

At the end of the school year I was promoted to the third grade and Billy stayed behind. I moved on and Billy didn't. I saw him less and less, until not at all. In my twenties, I heard Billy had died. I didn't get to go to the funeral. But later I was walking through the cemetery and saw a grave adorned with six small John Deere tractors. I went over and stood in silence thinking about Billy, how little he seemed to understand, how little the class understood him, and his early death. Standing there, I felt a deep sorrow wash over me. For a moment we shared the dark waters of the river beyond. Then I saw it, each tractor from the largest to the smallest was named: Washington; Adams; Jefferson; Madison; Monroe; and Adams.

Billy's been gone two-thirds of a century now, but he remains alive in my memories. Is he still plowing "a field somewhere?"

GRACIE'S CATERPILLAR
By Leslie Schult

He was still there on the railing,
Just crawling along his way.
Gracie had carefully placed him there
Protecting him from grown up steps
Or the sniffing of Jake's brown nose.
She watched as his furry little legs carried him away.

She did the same for the little cream colored moth
Who took a ride on the party boat with us.
When we got off on the island
She found the first green leaf of a blueberry bush
And placed him safely in his new home.

Gracie watches out for all the little creatures.
She says she wants to grow up to be a vet one day.
She has the makings of a fine professional,
A gentle kind heart and years to find her way.

WEDDING WALTZ, WITHOUT THE MAN
By Marsha Mathews

My daughters are getting married.
Or so they say.

In my pearls & lacy white lingerie,
they swish & sway.
Snapped around their beaming faces,
the elastic of half slips
plumps their cheeks;
satin drapes their hair.
Before them, tiny fists clutch celery stalks
Such solemn poise,
leaves turn lilac.
They down each step:
    left foot,
        right foot;
          left foot,
           right foot.

"You can't get married without a man," I say, laughing.
Taking my hands, they proceed to teach me
"the marriage waltz!" the eldest chimes.
"Of our new fam-i-ly!" the three-year-old chortles,
lifting her leg high, celery slipping,
the room rocking white as we stomp & whirl.

Previously published in Hallelujah Voices, (Aldrich Press)

THE BEST DAMN TITLE IN THE WORLD
By Ben Humphrey

"Doctor Humpfie," Sally cried as she ran down the hall of 2 East ahead of her mother. She stopped to give me a smile and a hug. A four-year-old Sally hugged me around my legs; and as was my habit, I got down on one knee so we were eye to eye. Holding up a new puzzle still in its cellophane wrapping, Sally exclaimed in delight, "I got a new puzzle."

"Good morning, Doctor Humphrey," Mrs. Carter said as she caught up with her daughter. She took Sally's hand and explained to her charming bald-headed daughter. "It's Monday, Sally. Doctor Humphrey will be very busy today. Maybe he can help you with that puzzle tomorrow."

Sally was one of the nurses' favorite patients. Ann came out of the nurses' station, received a hug from Sally, then led Sally and her mother to their room.

In July of 1964, I was a commissioned officer in the U.S. Public Health Service assigned as a clinical associate to 2 East, the children's leukemic ward at the National Institutes of Health (NIH) in Bethesda, Maryland. At that time, chemotherapy could induce a bone marrow remission in over ninety percent of children with acute lymphocytic leukemia. Thereafter, we were giving children in remission a monthly five-day course of intravenous chemotherapy to prevent a relapse.

On that morning, Sally was admitted for her third course of therapy. During her first admission to my service in July, we worked on a puzzle together to break the ice and continued putting puzzles together during her second monthly admission in August.

A bone marrow aspiration was performed on all patients before chemotherapy was begun. After this necessary but painful procedure, I carried my sobbing Sally back to her room, lay her down on the bed and pulled a sheet over her legs and chest. I sat on the edge of her bed; she let me hold one hand and with her free hand wiped the last tears away. Mrs. Carter knew the routines of this first day of admission to 2 East and that in less than an hour the results of the marrow would be available.

The news was good. An hour later, we learned the bone marrow aspirate did not contain any leukemic cells. Sally recovered from the trauma procedure and greeted me with a "Doctor Humpfie."

"We've been working of the proper pronunciation of your name, Doctor Humphrey" Mrs. Carter said.

To keep Sally from feeling she was being ignored, I picked her up, sat down in the extra chair with Sally on my lap and said, "Please don't do that." I explained that I had already acquired titles that I was required to use or respond to. "I enjoy my relationship with Sally and like her special title. To hear Sally cry out, 'Doctor Humpfie' brightens my day."

"Titles can be boring," I explained to Mrs. Carter. "I remember the first time I was called 'Doctor Humphrey' as a medical student, Pretty neat, I thought. The novelty soon wore off, and the title, Doctor, generally meant a demand was going to be placed on my time. Then, there was 'Herr Doktor' during my post-doctoral year in Germany." Smiling wryly, I told Mrs. Carter, "The Germans take titles very seriously."

Being called "sir" bothered me. "Recently I've heard 'sir' used in addressing me. I thought you had to be forty to be addressed as sir," I added.

After I had finished all that, Mrs. Carter explained, "Sally doesn't call you 'Doctor Humpfie' when we're at home. You're her 'Puzzle Doctor'."

"Wow!" I gave Sally a little hug. "That's great! You know, Sally, someday I hope to be a teacher at a medical school. Do you know what I'm going to have painted on my office door?"

Sally smiled and shook her head.

Then in a solemn tone I said. "G. Bennett Humphrey, M.D., Ph.D., S.C.P.D."

Mrs. Carter kept the verbal game going and asked. "What does S.C.P.D. stand for?"

I turned to Sally and said, "S.C.P.D. stands for," then tapping her four times lightly on the chest, "Sally - Carter's - Puzzle - Doctor."

Mrs. Carter laughed, Sally smiled as I nodded.

That evening driving home, I mused over my day. I was renting a small cottage on an estate in rural Maryland. The estate included not only the main house and my cottage, but also a barn and a fenced-in field where I kept a thoroughbred mare I was training. My other companion was a black Labrador.

When I got out of the car, my dog ran up wagging her tail and the thoroughbred trotted up to the fence and nickered. I liked and appreciated these bucolic forms of address. It was a pleasant way to end the day, just as "Doctor Humpfie" had been a wonderful way to begin it.

DADDY'S LITTLE GIRL
By Beckie A. Miller

She sits embraced upon his lap, her long blonde tresses splayed out across his chest. Her eyes continually dancing, as they dart back and forth between the book he reads to her and the television program that divides her attention with its noisy and colorful allure. She stops momentarily to brush a stand of hair impatiently from her eyes, anxious not to miss anything. No matter how many times he reads the story, it is never enough. She wants more of his undivided attention before the inevitable bedtime approaches. I watch this tender moment and wish I could paint it exactly how it is, a memory to keep forever etched in the colors of love.

This set of Virgos, father and child. So different now, but as they grow — as she grows up — as they share more of these times — they will meld into one another. The best of each of them will merge as each one changes the other and imparts their own uniqueness and views.

Earlier this evening, she grabbed her own little feed bucket and raced to keep up with Daddy's long legs. He was in a hurry to finish the evening chores and make sure all the horses were fed before dinner. She wanted more of their precious time together, never enough as she soaks it up like a thirsty sponge. Waddling along behind him she dumped her mini-bucket of feed into the barrel, missing half, then bending over to pick up the strays piece by piece, ever so slowly. Is it her ploy to suspend time — to keep his attention longer, to share her daddy-time forever? It is never enough for this young child and she pitches a fit each time it ends. *"No, not yet Daddy!"* is what her screams mean, before she learns the words to express it herself. Once she learns the words, a tantrum will no longer be necessary.

Oh dearest child, but could it only last forever. If the pleasure-filled times were always, they would become just another moment and not a memory worth painting -- worth prolonging. It was just yesterday that you were a tiny infant, seemingly tinier in his large and calloused hands -- those hands that held you gently and timidly then, as if you might break. His hands now play rough, in comparison, as you engage in tumbling matches, riding on his back playing *horsie*, and catch with

104

your ball. You do not understand it cannot last forever, and he understands fully it doesn't. He raised one son and one daughter already — who now raises her sons. He knows. Knowing makes him more patient and teaches him to give her a few more of his busy minutes unselfishly. He understands time stands still for no one, not even this precocious child.

For the two who claimed his heart first, he gained more to share with her. These moments change so quickly and many never to be again. He will enjoy them all both good and bad. Each has its place in the whole. Each are teachers with a message to impart upon her consciousness — her soul of humanity.

A father must divulge to a daughter the secrets of life that will take the child to adulthood properly with love and so much more. The child in return keeps him young at heart, vulnerable and sweetly tender, taking the edge off his anger, softening his grief from the loss of his son — his firstborn. He is her hero. She is his child, a special gift from God sent to him five years after the death of his son to teach him how to laugh and trust in life again, through the eyes of newfound fatherhood -- Daddy and daddy's little girl.

STARE DOWN
By Jim Gustafson

At seven, Zeda is already a scientist,
her attention spans the smallest moving thing with a patience that defies
her years.

It is the day before her parents will take her away to live we walk
together around the man made pond
that exaggerates the meaning of our waterfront home.

Alligator's wide eyes watch us, as we stop her small hand in mine. We
stare. "Don't blink," she orders, in a most serious tone,
taking charge of the situation, as she has done since the delivery room.

We stand together hand and hand, a sculpture, old man and a child,
so still, birds contemplate landing. Without a ripple, the gator moves,
swims out, and submerges with a stealth envied by the Navy's finest
engineers.

Zeda, mustering all the joy of childhood shouts to the gator, "We won,"
then, drops my hand, throws her arms around my waist, leans back,
looks up into my face and speaks words that move the axis of the earth,
change the tides forever—"I'll miss you Grandpa."

AT THE READING
By Carolyn Ingram, Ed.D, PCC

The auditorium is half full.
We've driven together, sit apart,
our daughter close to the stage.
It is hard to see her as sixteen;
clear to my heart
is how she was at four. We shared
one seat, she relaxed on my lap,
her hair rose-water fragrant.

Tonight Sarah's mom sits with us.
She rises from beside my husband
moves toward her daughter
perched next to mine. *Don't*
I want to say. The girls are away
from us not by will or rebellion,
just away, like weaning kittens.
Sarah's mom returns, eyes glazed.
That was a mistake, she whispers.
We half-smile. Grief rises,
the tide recedes. What's revealed
not for the first time: our daughters
have their own lives.

The poet takes her place,
spotlighted. I fall into her voice,
watch the girls, taken back to poems
I wrote when I was sixteen.
She reads her last to a hushed room.
We approach the girls' huddle in the lobby.
But even as the words slip out,
I know I should take the advice
I didn't give Sarah's mom.
Shall we get her autograph? I ask,

a tradition begun when she was five.
She dismisses me with a wave of hand
not unkind, just true to who she is now.
I can't grasp it through the passage of years
I wear for warmth like a sweater.

Her father drives us home.
I apologize. *I acted like a mom.*
She laughs, *But Mom, you are one.*

BECAUSE OF YOU
By Carol Bullman

When I'm with you, Baby, I wake up to morning's freshest light.
A hand squeezes mine when I walk downstairs, because of you.
When I'm with you, Baby, I have someone to hug in parking lots.
Strangers smile at me, because of you.
When I'm with you, Baby, I get to look at picture books.
I dance and clap, because of you.
When I'm with you, Baby, I bend down to smell flowers.
I soar high in swings, because of you.
When I'm with you, Baby, I admire the moon.
I sing during thunderstorms, because of you.
When I'm with you, Baby, I watch an angel sleep.
Happiness whooshes through me, because of you.
When I'm with you, Baby, everything is bright and new.
I am beginning again, because of you.

FISHING LESSON
By Gayla Chaney

I saw him standing on my pier in the soft heat of early morning as I went to pour my first cup of coffee. How long had he been standing there, his pole dipped in the lake, his tackle box beside him, calmly fishing off my pier like he owned the place? The sun was barely up, as was I, but this kid was wide awake and obviously had been for awhile, enjoying an early June morning before the temperature climbed to the forecasted ninety degrees. Perched on my dock, he appeared ready to reel in his catch of the day.

I could tell at a glance the boy was a Munson, and that galled me all the more. That Munson bunch produced nothing but lowlifes. I'd had plenty of run-ins with them in the past. And now, here was a young nephew or cousin of the Munson clan - a Munson for sure, based on the unmistakable stance that seemed a peculiar, inherited trait in that family. They were hefty in size and carried their weight on their heels with their toes pointed outward, producing a sort of waddle-walk. If they weren't moving forward, they seemed incapable of standing still. They would rock back and forth on their feet as I could see the boy doing now out on my pier.

Half the Munsons ended up in prison; the other half should have, in my opinion. They were a worthless crew who regularly lied and cheated, and it was rumored that some even beat their wives. They let their properties go. Their yards were usually cluttered with broken-down cars and bicycles and discarded furniture. Head lice, pink eye, impetigo regularly appeared at the schools via the Munson tribe.

And now, one of their offspring had the nerve to fish on my property without any regard for my rights or privacy. Though the trespasser was a child, he was still a Munson and that was enough to get me riled. I'll handle this, I thought, and set my coffee cup on the kitchen counter before heading out the back door.

The boy, probably ten or so, stood barefoot in cut-off jeans and no shirt. His flip flops were beside his tackle box along with a wadded up T-shirt. As I approached, I saw that he had something on his line. The tug and pull of a fish gave the boy a start, and he let out a whoop as he jerked his pole back. I stopped and watched as the kid skillfully reeled in a black bass, probably a seven-pounder.

"Get a load of that, would ya?" The boy hollered gleefully. I don't know if he even saw me. His exclamation was a self-congratulatory remark. For a moment, I didn't speak. Let the kid have his private victory party, I thought, watching the youngster dangling his catch and laughing at his prize. "You're a beaut! A keeper for sure," he was saying to the fish. He turned then and saw me watching him. I thought he might feel embarrassed or ashamed, having been caught fishing off a stranger's pier. But the boy was just too excited to feel anything else.

Grinning, he held up the bass for my inspection. "I caught this beauty all by myself. I bet I could catch one for you, too, if you'd like me to." The boy paused briefly for my response.

"Well, I don't..." I began.

"How much you think this baby weighs?" he interrupted me as he appeared to study the glistening fish.

"Hmmm. Maybe six or seven pounds," I offered in a lackluster tone. The kid shook his head at my guess.

"Bigger than that. I'm betting eight." He acted as though he were scanning a scale as he spoke in an authoritarian tone. As I watched this enthusiastic youth take the fish off his hook, I could tell that he was imitating somebody.

"You a Munson?" I blurted out. I had to verify my suspicions, remembering my reasons for coming out here. He was fishing off my pier, after all. I had the right to know.

"Yep," he answered casually without glancing up from his task. "Did you see me bring him in? He was a fighter for sure, but he was no match for me. I'm a bona fide angler. Do you know what that means?" he asked, but he didn't wait for my answer. "It means I'm a real fisherman like my granddad. He taught me how to do this," the boy said, motioning to his tackle and gear. "You want me to show you how? I'll teach you to catch an even bigger fish than this. You got a pole or you want to borrow mine?"

I stood there speechless for a second, sizing up my uninvited guest. "Just you show me," I replied. The young trespasser beamed when I said that and he quickly fixed a fat night-crawler on his hook. After a moment, he threw his line back into the water, his gaze intent on the spot in the lake where his bobber floated.

The boy reeled in the excess line, taking up the slack while pulling slightly to his right, rocking gently on his heels like a true Munson. "I'll show you what you need to do first. Watch and learn." He grinned and winked, contorting his face in a comical fashion causing me to chuckle.

110

"Shhhh," he whispered. "We don't want to scare the fish." He nodded his head in the direction of the lake where the morning sunlight was reflecting off the water. Despite the fact that my coffee was waiting back in my kitchen, growing colder by the second while I stood beside the trespassing angler on my pier, I couldn't move. Instead, I watched in silence like a neophyte taking in the moment as this confident, young Munson demonstrated his fishing techniques, certain if I were paying attention, I could absorb the lesson he was so generously willing to share.

FOSTERING BETTER THAN GARDEN-VARIETY GROWTH
By Ruth Sabath Rosenthal

The plant needs water and mulch
to grow strong live long
this child needs milk
loves ice cream too much
concedes to vitamins
for living strong long

the plant needs sunshine
this child needs sun-block in sunshine

the plant needs temperate climate
this child needs temperate home climate

the plant needs attention daily
or will wither and die
this child needs love
and attention daily
or by and by
will wither and fail

PARADISE
By Jasminne Mendez

Prologue

The school faces away from Eden St. pretending to reject the possibility of paradise. Its old brick walls are covered with black soot as if the Angel of Death himself had tried to enter and gotten trapped on his way. The main entrance and the parking lot rest silently in their government funded graves and the school, tired and lazy wants nothing to do with Eden. But Eden St. knows that within the school, lie tiny instruments of hope that give even me and this neighborhood a purpose.

I have Scleroderma, a chronic auto-immune disease that should have landed me in a bed collecting disability years ago. But instead, on Thursdays, I park my car on Eden St and walk up the street to a neighborhood elementary school where I spend three hours of my day teaching third and fourth graders how to think and write creatively. It's not often easy, but I make them work as hard as my medicine does to keep my own mind and body from falling over.

What I find most difficult about Thursdays is not the tiring half a block walk my legs struggle to get through like a 10K marathon, or standing for three hours straight without a bathroom break. What I find difficult is the fact that I have to park on Eden St. in a neighborhood that looks and feels nothing like a utopia.

The houses on Eden St. aren't ugly, but they aren't really anyone's home either. They are temporary solutions to a generation of welfare, Medicaid and food stamps. The houses are quaint ideas, with dogs that bark behind broken fences, and old toothless men that sit in pick-up trucks drinking lukewarm hope out of brown paper bags. The trees on Eden St. line the sidewalk and tower over the tiny 1940's houses that yearn to provide shelter and comfort but only manage to loom over windows and hug emptiness instead. Gardens don't grow on Eden St. Flowers bud during the early morning mist and low rider fumes wilt them during the night. Lilies and roses can only be found etched on the back of Maria's leg or as a symbol of stolen beauty on Esperanza's shoulder blade. Here, children are born to children and grandmothers raise them.

It's always cloudy on Eden St. At seven in the morning when I park my car, and eat my fast-food breakfast the grayness hovers over the cul-de-sac and fogs my windows. And still, at eleven am, when I walk back to my car after wrestling with the minds of bored children, I see that the sky has only barley shifted slightly to the right still dark and cold, the sun barely peeking through old yellow laced curtains sewn by someone's *abuela*. The street signs manage to stand tall and graffiti-less but that doesn't stop the mothers who drop their children off in the morning from rushing back into their houses, avoiding eye contact and conversation with anyone nearby

Eden St. in the ghetto. Adam and Eve in my third and fourth grade classrooms, sitting in plastic chairs, brown skin glowing, naked eyes, and innocent minds waiting to be tempted by my knowledge. Yet, I can only offer them a piece of paper, a pencil and an idea, the rest is up to them. Like a snake, I will slither in and out of their lives, teasing them with notions of a brighter future, opening the world to them one page at a time.   I will offer them one red apple, and in return they will feed me for the rest of my life, teaching me what the world is really like: gunshots at three in the morning, uncles and fathers in prison until November, hooker moms, ice cream trucks, and taco stands. Again, I smile when they tell me their unbelievably real stories, when I read their raw poetry and when Juan raises his hand and says: "Miss, we don't play PlayStation and watch TV all day because we want to, it's because *Mami* says it's not safe outside." And I swallow my words, choking on every judgmental phrase I ever uttered, and I do the only thing teachers do best, I change the subject. For the last six months I have misunderstood these tiny people. I have assumed that they lacked an imagination because they willingly gave it away. In reality, they've merely placed it on the top back shelf of their minds, only grabbing from it when they know someone will be there to help them.

And I do my best to help them, but it is hard for me at times. Most days I don't have the energy I should. I let the physical pain overpower my desire and passion to help them grow as writers and individuals. I stop writing on the board when I shouldn't because my shoulders give out. I sit down during a lesson when I know I should be walking around inciting creativity and ensuring that each child gets the attention he/she deserves. I become selfish and self-absorbed, begging God to numb my body in the middle of a read-aloud or revision session.

On this particular morning my arthritic bones ache, my muscles are sore with the pain of a body builder, and my skin is thick and swollen like a ripe mango ready to burst. I am out of breath after acting out a scene from a story. The children laugh. I want to keel over and die. I am so exhausted, but the children keep laughing. My grief is only noticeable and bearable to me.

The third grade students ask me to read the story again, they say: "Miss, you're really good at that." All the while I'm thinking, "Dear God, please pick me up, take me out of my skin and release the pain into nothingness." But He doesn't, and the children, still smile waiting for me to make words bloom like flowers from my lips. But all that I am able to release is a tired sigh, and a lie: "I'll read it again next week, but only if you earn it."

I convince them to start writing and I do my usual rounds, peering over shoulders, reading misplaced emotions and desperately spelled words. Suddenly, as I slyly massage my left thigh, the muscle throbbing, my little helper tugs at my shirt and points to a poem on his desk. This poem is the first thing he's written all school year:

Ai lob mai mom
She es preti
She es like da sun
Ai lob mai mom

Now I smile. "Thank you," I tell him. "Does it have a title?" He stares at his paper, thinking deeply, but he doesn't reply. I wait, patiently knowing that he's still trying to process the question. What's the title?" I ask again.

"I love my mom," he replies, reading the first line of the poem. "Do you like it?" he asks, his teeth edging out of his mouth, smiling and eager to please.

I nod, "It's one of the best poems I've read all year. I really like the simile you used. Can I read your poem to the class?" He smiles and nods, then puts his head down on his desk. He is embarrassed but proud as I read his poem to the class. I've suddenly lost track of the aches and pains, my dry cracked hands and arms still open and exposed seem irrelevant and small compared to the boy's teeth. For a moment I feel like the child's mother: nurturing, in love, and hopeful. I become light headed during the reading, and suddenly everyone claps. It's over. Four lines of truth that have become more real than all the pain I've felt the last nine months. The boy giggles. I squeeze his shoulder and finally release the pain that has been pulsating through my body. It is euphoric. It is in that moment that I no longer find it difficult to park on Eden St in the ghetto, because I understand that the houses, and the dogs, and the trees, and the clouds, and my illness don't matter. On Thursdays Eden St. *is* paradise because *these* children can make even *my* worst day feel like a miracle.

SLEEP TIGHT, MY LITTLE DARLING
By Lynn C. Johnston

Sleep tight, my little darling
May your dreams take off in flight
As you cuddle to your pillow
Your face glows softly by night-light

I kiss your forehead gently
As to not disturb your dreams
Maybe you could bring me back
A rainbow or some moonbeams

Sleep tight, my little darling
May your dreams be just as sweet
As the child here before me
Nestled gently in the sheets

Previously published in *Angel's Dance:*
A Collection of Uplifting & Inspirational Poetry (Whispering Angel Books)

Sandra Ervin Adams is listed in *A Directory of American Poet & Writers* and has been published in anthologies and literary journals. In 2006 she authored a poetry chapbook, *Union Point Park Poems,* and in 2011, *Through A Weymouth Window.* She has been a writer-in-residence at Weymouth Center for the Arts and Humanities in Southern Pines, NC. Sandra lives near the North Carolina coast.

Francine L. Baldwin-Billingslea is a mother, a grandmother, a breast cancer survivor and a second time around newlywed who has recently found a passion for writing. In the last five years, she has had several publications in the Whispering Angels and Chicken Soup for the Soul anthologies, as well as in magazines and online. She has also written an inspirational memoir titled, *Through it all and out on the other side,* which can be purchased through Amazon.com, BarnesandNoble.com and Xlibris.com. She loves writing, traveling, and spending quality time with her loved ones, especially with her grandchildren.

Julie G. Beers has written for multiple television series including *Walker, Texas Ranger, Renegade* and *Gene Roddenberry's Earth: Final Conflict.* She is a freelance writer and editor, and currently works as a researcher at AFI (American Film Institute) on the AFI Catalog of Feature Films. Julie has the privilege of traveling to many different worlds whenever she plays with her young niece and nephew. "Giant Black Widow Spider Island" is dedicated to Bijan and Sophia, two of this world's most imaginative, daring and fun kids.

James Bettendorf After retiring from teaching math for 34 years, he was accepted for a two-year poetry internship on the Loft Master Track program in Minneapolis, Minnesota, which he completed in 2009. His grandchildren provide a rich trove of material for writing. He has had poems published in *Off Channel, Main Channel Voices, Light Quarterly, Rockhurst Review, Ottertail Review, Talking Stick Vols. 18-20, Verse Wisconsin* and *Free Verse.* He has also been published in an anthology,

Gathering, with the other graduates of the "Forward" poetry program at the Loft.

Jane Blanchard divides her time between Augusta and St. Simon's Island, Georgia. Her poetry has appeared in many journals and magazines as well as in the anthologies *Cradle Songs, Dogs Singing* and *Shout Them From the Mountaintops II*.

Kellye Blankenship is a servant to a husband and five children. She enjoys sneaking of to her tiny office in the woods where she dives into fantasy and fun reality, with an occasional dip into serious writing. Her works can be seen in *Living Lessons, Nurturing Paws* and she writes a weekly article entitled *A Day in Education*. She has recently completed her first short story book titled *Silent Screams of an Abused Child*. This book is a non-fiction story of a childhood that begs to be forgotten and should be available soon for purchase. kellyeblankenship@ymail.com http://web.mac.com/kellyeblankenship

Ann Reisfeld Boutté is a writer of poetry, essays, and feature stories. Her work has appeared in many publications including *The Southern Poetry Anthology Volume IV, Texas Poetry Calendars, Wingbeats: Exercises & Practice in Poetry*, and *The Weight of Addition*. She has a Master's Degree in journalism and has worked as a feature writer for a daily newspaper and a national wire service. She was a Juried Poet in the Houston Poetry Fest in 2001, 2005, 2009, and 2010.

Carol Bullman is the author of *The Christmas House* (Ideals Children's Books, 2008). She lives and writes in Texas, where her husband and their two boys supply a constant stream of ideas and motivation for her stories, essays, and poems. www.carolbullman.com.

Gayla Chaney lives and writes in central Texas. Her fiction has appeared in *Potomac Review, Concho River Review, Natural Bridge, Cicada, Thema, Carve, U.S. Catholic, 34*[th] *Parallel* and *Nurturing Paws*. When not writing, Gayla likes to collect street junk and transform it into something delightful.

Elayne Clift, a writer and journalist in Saxtons River, Vt., is a Vermont Humanities Council Scholar and an adjunct lecturer in English and Gender Studies. The author of several books of poetry and short fiction and editor of three anthologies, her first novel, *Hester's Daughters*, based on The Scarlet Letter, has just been published. She is currently working (with Christine Morton) on a book about doula-supported birth in the US. (www.elayne.clift).

Daawy Her essay about the children of Mali's addictive smiles is very close to her heart. She is the proud mother of two lovely children and wife to a very supportive husband. She won a writing competition as a child when she had to write a 'miss you' letter, and she addressed her letter to God. This is the first time she has had her writing published, and she is truly grateful for this golden opportunity. She likes to search for optimism in the cold coves of despair. This ray of light motivates all her writings. Please follow her at http://twitter.com/Daawy or visit her at http://daawy.blogspot.com/

Barbara Kay Daniel's inspirational publications include *Woman's World, Fate* and numerous international magazines. She won her first poetry award at age 16 from *Ingenue*, and, recently honorable mention from *Writer's Digest*. Her publications include dozens of short stories, poems, a conceptual dance suite, and a commercial production of *Marching to Georgia*, her full-length play, in NYC. *Batbrains*, her one-act play won first place, then published by Samuel French, Inc. She holds a B.F.A from Virginia Commonwealth University, and also studied Interarts at Hunter. She resides in Buffalo Junction, VA, enjoys portrait painting, and networks on Facebook and Kencat95@aol.com.

Holly Day is a housewife and mother of two living in Minneapolis, Minnesota who teaches needlepoint classes in the Minneapolis school district. Her poetry and fiction has recently appeared in *Hawai'i Pacific Review, The Oxford American*, and *Slipstream*, and she is a recent recipient of the Sam Ragan Poetry Prize from Barton College. Her book publications include *Music Composition for Dummies, Guitar-All-in-One for Dummies*, and *Music Theory for Dummies*, which has recently been translated into French, Dutch, Spanish, Russian, and Portuguese.

Liz Dolan is a five-time Pushcart nominee, who has won an established artist fellowship from the Delaware Division of the Arts. Her second poetry manuscript, *A Secret of Long Life*, which is seeking a publisher, was nominated for the Robert McGovern Prize. Her first poetry collection, *They Abide*, was recently published by March Street Press.

Terri Elders, LCSW, lives near Colville, WA with two dogs and three cats. A lifelong writer and editor, Terri's stories have appeared in dozens of periodicals and anthologies, including two previous editions of Whispering Angel books. Her latest project is co-creating anthologies for the new *Not Your Mother's Book* series for Publishing Syndicate. She is a public member of the Washington State Medical Quality Assurance Commission. Contact her at telders@hotmail.com. She blogs at http://atouchoftarragon.blogspot.com/.

Karen Etheldattar is the author of three volumes of poetry: *Earthwalking & Other Poems*, *Thou Art a Woman & Other Poems* and *Steam Rising Up from the Soul*, and four chapbooks: *The Bambini Chronicles*, *The Cat Poems*, *Woman Artists & Woman as Art*, and *Poems of Peace & Protest*. Her poems have been published in *WomanSpirit*, *Off Our Backs*, *Dark Horse*, *Calyx*, *Northwest Magazine*, *The Christian Science Monitor*, and Papier Mache Press anthologies, *If I Had My Life to Live Over, I'd Pick More Daisies*, and *At Our Core: Women Writing About Power*. She can be reached at Ethelsdatr@aol.com.

Cona F. ("Faye") Gregory-Adams is an award-winning writer of poetry, children's books, nonfiction, and short fiction. She is now serving as Missouri's Senior Poet Laureate 2012. Published in newspapers, magazines, poetry journals and anthologies in the USA, UK, Korea and Canada, Faye also served as Missouri's Senior Poet Laureate in 2010, and was a featured poet in *Lucidity Poetry Journal*, summer of 2011. View her work at www.fayeadams.com, or email her at writer@fayeadams.com.

Carol L. Gloor is a semi-retired attorney, writing for forty years, mostly poetry. Her work has appeared in many print and online journals and anthologies, most recently in the magazine *Christian Century*; print journals *Sow's Ear*, *Slant*, and *Exit 13* ; the anthology *A Bird in the Hand: Risk and Flight*, and in the online journal *Stymie: a Journal of Sport and Literature*. She is a member of the Chicago poetry collective Egg Money Poet at eggmoneypoets.org.

R'becca Groff is a former administrative assistant turned freelance/creative writer who enjoys writing both fiction and non-fiction stemming from her native Iowa small town upbringing. She currently writes a business column for the *Cedar Rapids Gazette* and contributes to a monthly column on Iowa's growing wine industry for the Dubuque, Iowa-based magazine, *Julien's Journal*. She is pursuing representation/publication for her women's fiction novel, *Iron Angel*, and enjoys blogging about life and all its conundrums that influence a writer's journey at http://rebeccasnotepad.wordpress.com. You can find her at www.Facebook.com/Rebecca.Groff as well as Linkedin.com (R'becca Groff).

Jim Gustafson graduated from Florida Southern College and received his master's degree from Garrett Theological Seminary at Northwestern University, in his hometown of Evanston, Illinois. Jim lives in Fort Myers, Florida, where he reads, writers and pulls weeds. His poems have most recently appeared in *Hektoen International Journal*, *10x10*,

Boxing Insider, Barefoot Review, and *Poetry Quarterly*.   His website is www.jimgustafson.com.

Ben Humphrey is a retired professor of pediatric oncology living in the Rocky Mountains. In 2005, he started writing and publishing poems. Most of his poems are influenced by Taoism, but a poem about his youth was included in Whispering Angel Books anthology, *Living Lessons*. In 2010, he started working on a memoir of his professional experiences caring for children with leukemia. A short story, Ralph, from his memoir, which his still being drafted, was included in *Nurturing Paws*. Comments on his work are welcomed via email: Ghumphreyb@aol.com

Carolyn Ingram is a psychologist and coach who helps others discover their next calling, and then do something meaningful with that calling. Her poetry appears in *Pelican Review, Living Lessons, California Quarterly, Marin Poetry Center Anthology*, and *The Prose-Poem Project* among others. She co-wrote the non-fiction books *Have You Ever Been a Child*, and *The Not-So-Scary Breast Cancer Book,* and has published flash fiction on-line at *BustOut*. She loves supporting others to live from the creative flow, in work and all creative pursuits. carolyn@carolyningram.com

Debbie Izzi spent fifteen years in international finance. Then she had twins. Now she lives in Napa, California in a big yellow house with her husband and three boys. She spends her days playing baseball, searching for snakes, applying band-aids and of course, writing stories for and about children.   An excerpt from her novel-in-progress, *The Misery Eaters*, won second place in the 2012 Alabama Writers' Conclave Juvenile Fiction Contest. She can be reached at: izzi.debbie@gmail.com.

Carolyn T. Johnson, a former banker and now freelance writer from Houston, Texas, draws on her colorful life experiences in the US, Europe and South Africa for her short stories, poetry and essays. She writes from the heart, the hurt, the heavenly and sometimes the hilarious. Her work can be found in *The Houston Chronicle* and *The Austin American-Statesman* newspapers, as well as *Hope Whispers, Living Lessons, Nurturing Paws, Chicken Soup for the Soul, Yale Journal of Humanities in Medicine* and other various anthologies and e-zines. She can be contacted at cetjohnson@comcast.net.

Roshanda Johnson graduated Summa Cum Laude from the University of Houston with a Bachelors of Science in Interdisciplinary Studies. She loves to slam, perform spoken word and act. She currently stars as Stephanie in the Gospella *The Divine Inheritance.* She has been published on *Say it at Your Wedding's* website and in *Pure Francis'* online literary journal, and has works appearing in the anthologies *American Society: What Poets See* and *Riversongs* later this year. She resides in Houston, Texas with her beloved dog Blue Belle.

Lynn C. Johnston is the author of *Angel's Dance: A Collection of Uplifting and Inspirational Poetry* and founder of Whispering Angel Books. Her poems and essays have been published in several anthologies, including *Forever Friends, Timeless Mysteries, Antiquities, The World Awaits,* and *Turning Corners, Bridges.* She served as editor for *Hope Whispers, Living Lessons, and Nurturing Paws.* Originally from New York, Lynn is a graduate of SUNY New Paltz. For more information, please visit www.whisperingangelbooks.com.

Jean L. Kaess is an award winning poet and journalist living in South Louisiana. She holds a Bachelor's degree in English with a concentration in Creative Writing from Nicholls State University in Thibodaux, LA. Her poem "Brigid's Forge II" appeared in *Hope Whispers.* Her freelance work also has appeared in *Sprinkles Magazine, eHow* and on numerous other websites. She is a mother, daughter, wife, and friend experiencing life as a 30-something in the "sandwich" generation of life. Jean can be reached through her blog at http://jeankaess.wordpress.com/.

Pamela L. Laskin is a lecturer in the English Department, where she directs the Poetry Outreach Center. Her poems and short stories have been published in numerous books and magazines. Her books include *Grand Central Station, Remembering Fireflies, Secrets of Sheets, Ghosts, Goblins, Gods and Geodes, Van Gogh's Ear,* and *Daring Daughters/Defiant Dreams.* She also co-authored *Animal Crackers and Their Friends.* Her published children's books include *A Wish Upon A Star, Historical Heroic Horses, Music From The Heart* and *The Buried Treasure.* She edited two collections: *The Heroic Young Woman* and *Life on the Moon: My Best Friend's Secrets.*

Mary Elizabeth Laufer is a freelance writer and substitute teacher in Saint Cloud, Florida. Her poems have been published in magazines, newspapers and several anthologies, including *Proposing on the Brooklyn Bridge* (Grayson Books, 2003), *Hunger Enough, Living Spiritually in a Consumer Society* (Pudding House Publications, 2004), *The Dire Elegies, 59 Poets on Endangered Species* (Foothills Publishing, 2006), *Bombshells, War Stories and Poems by Women on the Homefront* (OmniArts, LLC, 2007), *Beautiful Women – Like You and Me* (BW Books, 2007), *Living Lessons* (Whispering Angel Books, 2010) and *Cradle Songs: An Anthology of Poems on Motherhood* (Quill and Parchment Press, 2012).

Tom Leskiw lives outside Eureka, California with his wife Sue and their dog Gypsy. He considers his explorations of the natural world with Gypsy to be among the highlights of the past 13 years. An avid birder, he is a member of the Association for the Study of Literature and the Environment (ASLE). His essays, book and movie reviews appear in print and online journals including *Adventum; Birding; LBJ: Avian Life, Avian Arts; The Motherhood Muse (1ˢᵗ place contest winner); Snowy Egret; Terrain.org; Watershed* and forthcoming in *Riverwind*. His monthly column appears at www.RRAS.org. and his website resides at www.tomleskiw.com

David MacWilliams lives in Alamosa, Colorado with his wife Pilar and their two children. He teaches writing, literature, and linguistics at Adams State University there. He received his MFA in Creative Nonfiction from Ashland University in August, 2011. He has published in *Pilgrimage* and has a recent essay at Mason's Road, http://www.masonsroad.com/issue-5/creative-nonfiction-issue-5/sound-waves/. He's now working on his first book, a collection of essays on fatherhood. He's delighted to be contributing to Littlest Blessings and can be reached at dcmacwil@yahoo.com.

Susan Mahan has been writing poetry since her husband died in 1997. She is a frequent reader at poetry venues and has written and self-published four chap books, *"Paris Awaits"*, 2001 *"In The Wilderness of Grief"*, 2002, *"Missing Mum"*, 2005, and *"World View"*, 2009. She joined the editorial staff of *The South Boston Literary Gazette* in 2002. She has been published in a number of journals and anthologies and loves writing poems about her grandchildren!

Suzanne Manning resides in Massachusetts with her husband her soul-mate of 16 years and her beautifully, creative 13-year-old daughter. She started out expressing herself through her writings as a young teenager; she enjoys writing true life stories of her life's experiences. She has been published in two newspaper articles, has written a children's book called *Tales from a New England Farmhouse* and has been appeared in the anthology, *Nurturing Paws*. Suzanne can be reached at Farmhouse59@comcast.net

Marsha Mathews has published three chapbooks of poetry: *Northbound Single-Lane* (Finishing Line Press, 2010), *Sunglow & A Tuft of Nottingham Lace* (Red Berry Editions, 2011), *and most recently, Hallelujah: Voices from the Hollow* (Aldrich Press). Author Silas House selected Marsha's novel excerpt "More than a Mess of Greens" as one of the top three fiction finalists for the 2012 Rash Awards. The story, her first published fiction, appears in *The Broad River Review*. Marsha teaches writing and literature at Dalton State College. She enjoys water sports and eating crab cakes. She raised two way cool daughters. And her granddaughter calls often to talk to her cats, Azure and Muse.

Rosemary McKinley began writing to both entertain and inspire others. Her book, *101 Glimpses of the North Fork and Islands* was released in 2009. Her short stories, essays, and poems have been published online by the *Visiting Nurse Association of Long Island* and in *Lucidity, LI Sounds, Clarity, canvasli.com, Peconic Bay Shopper, Fate Magazine, Examination Anthology, Wormwood Press, Newsday*, and *The Poet's Arts*. Her Y/A historical novella, *The Wampum Exchange*, can be found on Amazon.com. She has been interviewed at KJOY, for the Suffolk Times and online.

Bridget McNamara-Fenesey lives in the Pacific Northwest, where she works as an independent business consultant when she is not pursuing her passion of writing. Bridget received her BA from the University of Notre Dame, and her JD from the University of Denver. She has been published in *The Sun* literary magazine, *Fate Magazine, Chicken Soup for the Soul*, as well as other local and national publications. She is thankful to her family for providing such a rich source of material for her muse. Bridget can be reached at bridgetmcnamara@comcast.net.

Jasminne Mendez is a performance poet, actress, teacher and published writer. She received her B.A. and M.Ed. from the University of Houston. She has performed her poetry in venues all around the Houston area and has shared the stage with respected writers and poets including Dagoberto Gilb, Sandra Cisneros and Taylor Mali. She has been published both nationally and internationally by Arte Public Press, the University of Chester, Telling Our Stories Press and in *Magnolia: a Journal of Women's Literature*. She is currently working on her first book length memoir and continues to promote literary events around the Houston area.

Beckie Miller began writing to vent the devastating pain from the death of her 18-year old son, Brian, who was robbed and killed in 1991. She is chapter-leader of Parents Of Murdered Children, in Phoenix, Arizona for the past twenty years and has won numerous awards for her work with crime victims. This is the third series of Whispering Angel Books she has had stories published in: Nurturing Paws and Living Lessons. She has also been published in *Every Woman has a Story, Dear Mom, I Always Wanted You to Know, Unsent Letters and The Arizona Republic*.

Jason Miller is an English Professor at North Carolina State University where he directs the teacher education program and teaches courses in twentieth-century American poetry. His poems have appeared in various journals including *Smartish Pace, The South Carolina Review, Whole Notes, Eclipse,* and *Plains Song Review.* He earned his MA degree from the University of Nebraska at Kearney and his Ph.D from Washington State University. In addition to publishing over a dozen articles, he is the author of *Langston Hughes and American Lynching Culture* (University Press of Florida 2011).

Harry P. Noble A native Texan, he spent two years in military service, eighteen months in Korea. His career was in computers, spending thirty years at the University of Houston and Lamar University. During that time, he earned a Bachelor's in mathematics and an MBA in finance. He retired in 1991. Returning to San Augustine, his hometown, he began writing biographical history for the newspaper, *The San Augustine Tribune.* That endeavor produced over a thousand articles and the publication of four books: *Texas Trailbrazers, As Noble as It Gets, Schools of San Augustine County: A History* and *Me and Burnice, A Simpler Time.*

Scott Peterson is a co-author of the book *Theme Explorations: a Voyage of Discovery.* His poems and essays have appeared in *The Plains Song Review, Beyond Forgetting: Poetry about Alzheimer's Disease, Home and Other Places, Catapult, Braking Ground, Nurturing Paws,* as well as other journals and magazines. He is a consultant for the National Writing Project and teaches writing classes at Western Michigan University. He lives in Mattawan, MI.

Sharon Medoff Picard is a social worker/psychoanalyst in private practice who lives and works in Westchester, County, New York. After years of thinking about writing, she joined a weekly writers' group and has been composing stories ever since.

Lynn Pinkerton is a freelance writer who knew in the fifth grade that she wanted to be a writer when she grew up. Sidetracked by careers in social services and special events marketing, Lynn eventually reclaimed her childhood aspiration, joined a writing group and began publishing. Her work has appeared in a variety of print and on-line publications including *The Christian Science Monitor, New Southerner* and *The Shine Journal,* as well as several anthologies including *Nurturing Paws, The Path* and *The Porch Swing.* She divides her time between New Chapel Hill and Houston, Texas.

Carol Rhodes lives in Houston, TX. Her creative works, short stories, personal essays, poetry, non-fiction articles, plays, and book reviews, have been widely published. Among her credits are *The Houston Chronicle, Christian Science Monitor, Stroud (England) News & Journal*, and *The Houston Press* newspapers; *Country Home, Good Old Boat* and *Texas* magazines. RE:AL, *Journal of Stephen F. Austin University*, book *Chicken Soup for the Girlfriend's Soul*, and numerous other publications. Additionally, Carol is a freelance literary and technical editor, business consultant, and instructor of her popular business writing courses, "Why Not Write It Right?" and "E-mail Protocol."

Ruth Sabath Rosenthal is a New York poet, well published in literary journals and poetry anthologies in the U.S. and abroad. In 2006, her poem *On yet another birthday* was nominated for a Pushcart prize. Ruth's full-length book, *Facing Home and Beyond*, published by Paragon Poetry Press, Inc., can be purchased online from Amazon.com, and from the publisher, via e-mail: paragonpoetry@aol.com: For more about Ruth, please feel free to "Google" her and visit her website: www.ruthsabathrosenthal.moonfruit.com

Leslie Schult is a writer, a poet, and a fiction writer of short stories and essays. Her work has been published in various local and regional newspapers such as *Walt Whitman Writer's Corner* and *The Women's Center of Huntington*. She participates and facilitates in writing workshops for women. She is also a Clinical Social Worker in private practice as well as a "practicing grandmother." Children inspire her with their rich observations and simplistic ideals; often reminding all of us of great truths such as *Gracie's Catepillar*. She takes great pleasure in telling their stories and is pleased to be part of this anthology.

Don Segal has been published in the *Deep Waters* anthology published by the Tall Grass Writers Guild in June, 2012, and the *Emily Dickinson Poetry Award* (Universities West Press) anthology as a semi-finalist. His other publication credits include *Miriam's Well* at www.miriamswell.wordpress.com, *Bottle Rockets, The Small Pond Magazine, Hummingbird* and *Blueline*. He has a blog at http://www.donsegal.wordpress.com that includes his drawings, photographs, poetry and discussion of anything that interests him! He lives in Guilford, CT with his wife and children.

Thanecha Senat is a health educator for a not-for-profit organization that works with adolescents in Brooklyn, New York. She holds a Masters in Community Health Education with specialization in Adolescent Health. Though she has no children of her own, she draws her inspiration for her writing from her niece, five nephews, five godchildren and life experiences. This is her first publication.

Elaine Dugas Shea, a New England native with love for the ocean, has lived in Montana for 40 years. She enjoyed a career in social justice working with American Indian Tribes and civil rights. Her poetry was featured in *Third Wednesday, South Dakota Review, Front Range Review, CAMAS, Spillway,* and several anthologies, including *The Light in Ordinary Things, Hope Whispers, When Last on the Mountain: The View from Writers over Fifty* and elsewhere. She thanks her children Deva & John for this story.

Deb Sherrer is a writer, psychotherapist, yoga instructor, and activist in violence prevention. She lives in Shelburne, Vermont with her husband and daughters. Her poetry has been published in *The Burlington Poetry Journal, The Mountain Troubadour, Vermont Woman, Affilia,* and *Violence Against Women International Journal.* More of her poetry, essays, and memoir can be read at: www.debsherrer.com.

Susan Siegel She has been writing poetry for almost 30 years. She writes about everyday happenings in life. She is a mother of two and has been married for almost 30 years. She tries to see beauty in everything around her and express her wonder of it all through her words.

Raven Sisco revels in the written word, both poetry and prose. As a poet, she has had poems published in college and adult literary journals, including *Rabbit* in Melbourne, Australia and *The Storyteller* in Arkansas. She has also won awards from various organizations including the National League of American Pen Women and the California Federation of Chaparral Poets, Inc. Currently starting her second year at San Jose State University, she is majoring in English, which she plans to teach at the high school level, and will continue to write both poetry and prose.

Janet Tamez is a writer and poet who grew up in the urban-Cuban culture of Union City, NJ. She takes on the world with the voice of dynamic women in her life such as her mom, Abuela, and sisters. As an advocate for young women, Janet has founded "The Young Goddess," a series of motivational workshops centered on goddess archetypes and women studies. Her short story, "Wherever you go, there you are," has been featured in Whispering Angel's *Living Lessons* anthology. Janet lives in Denver, Colorado where she serves as a Creative Writing instructor for high school students.

Paula Timpson She is a mommy and published poetess. Her poetry "Spirit" series books are available on Amazon. http://paulaspoetryworld.blogspot.com. Her son is her Forever Muse! She writes poetry everyday for God's glory!

Tina Traster is a *New York Post* columnist, a Huffington Post blogger and an essayist. She is the author of *Burb Appeal Too and Hits & Misses: New York Entrepreneurs Reveal Their Strategies*, a compendium of her columns from *Crain's New York Business*. Her work has appeared in newspapers, magazines, literary journals and on NPR. Her essays have been anthologized in literary collections *Living Lessons, Nurturing Paws*, and *Mammas and Pappas*. Traster is writing a memoir about her adopted Russian daughter that is due out next year.

Carolyne Van Der Meer is a Montreal journalist and PR practitioner who lectures in McGill University's Public Relations program in Montreal, Canada. Her poetry and short fiction have been published in journals and anthologies in Canada, Italy and Ireland, including *Ars Medica, Bibliosofia, Boyne Berries, Can Can, Canadian Woman Studies, Carte Blanche, Crannóg, Helios* and *the WOW!* Anthology among others, and is forthcoming in Ireland's *Windows 20* anthology. She holds undergraduate and graduate degrees in English literature and also recently completed a graduate certificate in Creative Writing at the Humber School for Writers in Toronto, Canada.

James Vasquez is a retired faculty member of the University of Washington. James writes Bible-based classic poetry and has published six books over the last four years. He has won numerous awards, including "Master Poet" from the Society of American Poets. His books are available from Amazon.com and from the publishers. Please visit his website at: http://jamesvasquez.tateauthor.com/

Louise Webster graduated with a B.A. in Communication Arts. Upon graduation, she worked at a cable T.V. station writing the evening news. Staying home, after the birth of her first child, she continued contributing work to many small presses and won a poetry contest celebrating the history of Lake Ronkonkoma. Louise also wrote for some of the more commercial magazines and anthologies. She wrote an article for *Garden Design*, a psychology text book, *Graces and Dog Blessings* by June Cotner, and is a frequent contributor to a science fiction quarterly.

N.K. Weddle is a freelance writer hailing from Independence, Missouri. Norman's fiction can also be found in the upcoming issue of *THEMA*,

Spring 2013 issue. *Liar, Liar, Pants on Fire* was inspired by a conversation with his grandson, Dane.

Cherise Wyneken is retired from teaching and raising four children and lives with her husband in Albany, CA. She began studying creative writing in mid-life and has since enjoyed sharing her prose and poetry with readers through a variety of journals, periodicals, anthologies, two books of poetry, a memoir of her spiritual journey, a novel, a children's spiritual fantasy, a children's audiocassette, two poetry chapbooks, and a nonfiction collection of stories from my life: *Stir-Fried Memories*, recently out from www.whisperingangelbooks.com A good part of her work is spiritually oriented. She currently writes a poetry column at www.examiner.com/poetry-in-oakland/cherise-wyneken   See also: http://www.authorsden/cherisewyneken